Keith

Hathaway House, Book 11

Dale Mayer

Books in This Series:

Aaron, Book 1

Brock, Book 2

Cole, Book 3

Denton, Book 4

Elliot, Book 5

Finn, Book 6

Gregory, Book 7

Heath, Book 8

Iain, Book 9

Jaden, Book 10

Keith, Book 11

Lance, Book 12

KEITH: HATHAWAY HOUSE, BOOK 11
Dale Mayer
Valley Publishing Ltd.

ISBN-13: 978-1-773363-82-0
Print Edition

About This Book

Welcome to Hathaway House. Rehab Center. Safe Haven. Second chance at life and love.

Keith came to Hathaway House at his sister's insistence. For he has already given up on regaining the future she keeps telling him that he can find here or, for that matter, any other future worth having. And, besides, don't they know he's too weak for the trip and for the treatment and for any of the plans the team has for him? Don't they know he's broken beyond repair, and nothing they can do will fix him?

But apparently they don't because no one listens to him. Not the doctors. Not his sister. And definitely not the tiny woman who keeps delivering his coffee at 5:00 a.m.

Ilse, head chef for Hathaway House, rarely ventures out of the kitchen she manages. It's easier to deal with the groceries and the staff than it is to see the pain and suffering of those she feeds. But something about Keith and his frailty calls to her. She can't help but go out of her way to ensure he has everything he needs. Even though she knows she cannot keep their relationship on a professional level, once started.

Even if not in her best interests to do so. Because, in this case, surely Keith's best interests matter, so much more than her own.

Sign up to be notified of all Dale's releases here!

https://smarturl.it/DaleNews

Chapter 1

KEITH CARRUTHERS STARED out the window. A storm raged outside as Mother Nature battled against the window glass in front of him. He lay in his bed, a bed new to him, in the room that was new to him also. Then again nothing was the same about his life right now. Except there wasn't a whole lot about it to like.

He didn't understand why he was here, except that his sister had made it sound like the perfect answer for him. All he could think about was that he shouldn't have bothered. It wasn't really like him to be this way, but this listless lack of spirit, not caring about anything, seemed to be the way of his world right now. He hated that because he had never had room for self-pity in his world before, but sometimes life knocked you down, and every time you got back up, you got knocked down again.

He knew the old maxim was to just keep getting up until you finally managed, but what should you do when you no longer cared to try? He'd had thirty separate surgeries on the one leg. Six other times they had operated to remove bits of shrapnel from his back, from his butt, and from his thighs.

He remembered waking up from one surgery and saying, "Doc, just kill me now."

The doctor had smiled, patted him on the shoulder, and said, "No way, not at this point. You are a work in progress, and we don't give up on those."

And he groaned and sank back under, and that had been six months ago.

Now he was here, and, so far, his sister Robin hadn't been told—or hadn't shown up at least. But then she worked downstairs in the vet clinic.

He smiled at that because his sister had always been a crazy animal lover, but then his smile fell away. He knew she worried about the animals in her care in a big way, and she worried about him too. It was hard to throw off depression when it sank into you. It dug in and ate the marrow from his very bones, leaving him with nothing but a lackluster viewpoint on everything around him.

He wasn't suicidal, thank God, though he knew that a lot of people around him worried about it. He also hated taking medication for something he shouldn't have to take medication for.

He'd always been physically fit, proud of his prowess, of his endurance, and of his strength—until all this happened. It was hardly fair that he got caught by an IED, but, then again, it wasn't fair that anybody did, and he certainly wasn't the first and wouldn't be the last. The only good thing was he'd been alone. Of course that also meant that he had laid out there for a long time until he got help. But, when help came, he got fast and effective medical aid. He was alive but couldn't count how many times over the last year or so he had wished he hadn't been. Only *wishing it* was a long way from doing something serious about it.

Just then a knock came at his door. He didn't even bother turning.

"Not even going to say hi to your sister?" Robin said gaily.

He lifted a hand and rolled over slightly, shuddering as the pain racked up and down his spine.

She noticed. She always noticed.

"Hey, sis," he said. "Why did you drag me here anyway?"

"You'll see," she said, with a determined cheerfulness.

But then that was her. She was all about sunshine and roses, doing what she could to help people and animals. He used to be like that, until he'd seen so much of the darkness in life that he wondered if humanity shouldn't have just been wiped off the planet instead. After all, the people had done very little *for* the planet Earth. Instead they had stripped it clean and kept busy finding other things we could profit from, like war.

He smiled as she walked toward him. "You still have that spring in your step, as if every day is a good day," he said.

She chuckled. "Every day *is* a good day," she said, then bent down gently, wrapped her arms around him, and gave him a kiss on his cheek. "Besides, I brought somebody with me."

"Oh, great," he said, "more happy-go-lucky people. Can't wait."

"Not so much," a woman said, her smooth, silky voice coming from the doorway.

He looked around his sister's arm to see a small woman, leaning against the door, her arms crossed over her chest. She was about five-four, maybe five-three, but her hair was long and loose and fell to her waist and beyond. He looked at her in surprise. "And who are you?"

"I told you that I brought somebody to meet you," Robin said. "She's our chef and works in the kitchen here."

He nodded slowly. "Well, that must be a job and a half."

She laughed. "I'm Ilse," she said with a smile. She walked closer and reached out a hand. "Nice to meet you."

Gradually he reached a hand out to her and said, "I'm Keith. Nice to meet you too."

She looked to the window at the storm raging outside. "Good thing we have nice warm meals in here."

"What's for dinner?" he asked, although no interest was in his tone because food was not something his body particularly liked anymore.

"Do you eat?" she asked, turning to study him.

He flushed slightly, realizing his sister had probably told her something about him.

"I didn't tell her anything," Robin said crossly before he could speak. "You always jump right to thinking I've revealed our family secrets or something."

He rolled his eyes. "I don't have much appetite," he said lightly.

Ilse looked at him with a smile and nodded. "I imagine all the medications and surgeries make that a little rough too."

"What goes in has to come out," he said, "and it's not always the smoothest journey."

Her lips quirked. "Isn't that the truth? So you're here, and it's day one for you," she said. "So have a relaxing day today, and tomorrow is getting to know your team and all. Can I bring you something from the kitchen for dinner?"

He looked at her in surprise. "I don't think a chef delivers the food," he said.

At that, she gave him a full-blown smile. "Well, nothing about this place is normal, or so I'm told. I deliver food all the time. And Dennis, the guy who thinks he runs the kitchen," she said with a smirk, "delivers food everywhere—

inside, outside, even down to the pastures. He's always on the go, trying to make people happy."

"No wonder Robin likes it here so much."

"Absolutely," Ilse said. She walked to the window and stared out.

As she turned, he realized her hair was slightly damp, which is probably why she wore it down, leaving it long and flowing so it could dry. He couldn't remember the last time he saw a woman with long hair like hers.

"We don't see this weather very often," she murmured.

"No," he said. "I was just thinking it matched my mood."

"Nah," Robin said brightly. "It's not nearly dark enough." He turned and glared at her, but she grinned impudently. "That look does not scare me," she said.

"Why not?" he asked. "It used to work well enough."

"It used to," she said. "That was a while back. Now? Not so much. Maybe because you use it so often."

He shrugged. "Whatever."

More commotion came at his door, and then somebody else walked in. The two women brightened.

"Hello, Dani. How you doing?" Robin asked.

"I'm doing fine," she said. "Just came to check up on your brother." Dani turned to look at him. "How are you doing, Keith?"

"Feeling a little worse for wear and wondering why my room is like Grand Central Station," he said.

At that, Dani chuckled. "You'll get used to it," she said. "Buck up. People are moving all over the place at this center."

"What about patient privacy?"

Robin protested. "Don't be so cranky."

"I'm always cranky," he snapped.

"No, you *were* always cranky," she said. "You're not allowed to be cranky here. Everybody here is full of niceness and humor."

"My world is not full of chihuahuas and birthday cake," he said. "It's full of rottweilers and death."

At that, Robin reached out and grabbed his fingers and clung to him.

He knew that she understood, but it wasn't fair to keep punching on her. He groaned. "See? You always made me cranky."

She burst out laughing, and a reluctant grin came to his lips.

"And I can never stay mad at you," he said with a half sigh. "You're just too nice."

The whole exchange between the two of them was witnessed by the other two women. Dani appeared way too young to be managing a place like this. Not only managing, according to his sister, but had started it in order to save her father. Though Ilse had really caught Keith's attention.

As she walked toward the doorway, her long hair bounced off her hips, coming halfway down her buttocks. He couldn't help but admire how trim and shapely they were too. He called out to her suddenly, "Thanks for coming by. Sorry I'm a bit of a bear today."

She looked at him in surprise, and then a gentleness crossed her face. "You're entitled, you know? Everybody gets to be dark and dangerous for a little while. Only when it goes on for a long time does it get to be too much." She lifted a hand, saying, "Later," and walked out. Dani stopped, turned to look at him, and whistled. "Ilse doesn't come out of her kitchen very often, so obviously you are special."

"Nah," he said, "that's just my sister. She's forever dragging people into my world. I think she's trying to save me or something."

"I wonder why that would be such a surprise," Robin said with a laugh. "There's only the two of us."

"I'm fine, you know?" he said slowly. In fact, they had more in the family, but the rest were half siblings that he didn't know—along with his father.

She looked at him, and her smile fell away. "No, honey, you're not. The doctors can only do so much to fix the outside, and I don't even know how to begin to fix the inside." And she squeezed his fingers again.

"I'm doing what I can do," he said, "one day at a time."

"And you can do that," she said, "but don't expect me to walk away. You can get as dark and as deep and as ugly as you want, but I'll still stand right here at your side. It's just the two of us, and I'm not letting you go. I've come close to losing you too many times, and, now that you're on the other side of all those surgeries, no way I'll let you go down that pathway just because we can't figure out how to heal your heart. *Yet.*"

"I'm not suicidal or anything. I've told you that," he said firmly.

"Good thing," she said, "or I'll put you in a padded cell and lock you up for life. You might not like it, but you'd still be alive, and I won't lose you." With that, she bent down, kissed him hard on the forehead, and stormed off.

But he still wasn't alone.

Dani studied him with a tiny smile playing at the corner of her lips. "You'll liven things up around here," she said smoothly.

"Well, that's not usually what somebody says to me," he

said, in surprise.

"Oh, I'm sure," she said. "But Robin is a pretty active person around here, and, now that she's with Iain, she's even more involved."

"I'm looking forward to meeting him," he said, "but I'd much rather be on my feet."

"Well, you can probably try crutches," she said, tapping the tablet in her hand. "But that may have to wait until you've recovered from your travels and after the team has worked up a full assessment."

"The last place did one assessment after another," he said. "Why does there have to be a new one all over again?"

She chuckled again. "Don't be so cranky," she said. "It's all good."

"It's all good from your side of life," he said. "It doesn't look so good from mine."

ILSE WISTBURY WALKED back into her kitchen, feeling the double doors close behind her with a sense of relief. She was so much more comfortable here in the kitchen than out there. She'd rather deal with food problems, cranky cooks, and temperamental equipment any day. Dealing with patients and the general public? Not so much.

This was her domain, and she was comfortable with every aspect of it. She could handle it alone if she had to, but she'd have to get up pretty early and limit the options a bit. Instead, she had seven full-time staff and another three who came in part-time, plus somebody who managed all her orders.

Speaking of which, Ricky came racing toward her, crying

out, "There's no lamb. There's no lamb."

She looked at him in surprise. "And?"

He stopped, took a deep breath, and said, "They shorted us on the lamb."

"Well, the lamb wasn't intended until tomorrow," she said. "When is the next order coming in?"

"Doesn't matter," he said, "because they won't have lamb tomorrow either."

"Okay. Then we don't have lamb," she said, shrugging.

"But they did give us extra cream," he said proudly. "The use-by dates were a little off, so I got them to knock the price in half and to add another four gallons."

"Good," she said with a smile. "Not exactly a replacement for lamb though."

"No," said Gerard, one of her cooks, from the other side of the kitchen island. "However, we're making fresh pasta, so why don't we whip up a walnut and cheese pasta dish with cream sauce?"

"That might work," she said, "but we certainly won't need four gallons for that."

"Cream puffs," one of the other guys called out.

"Panna cotta," somebody else suggested.

"All good ideas," she said. "Let's see if we can work them into the menus." She turned to Gerard. "We probably don't need very much of the cream for the pasta. You just want to make it," she teased. "You love making fresh pasta."

"Absolutely I do," he said. "You know fresh pasta is the best *any*time, but, if we need to make up for the missing lamb, then let's make it that one."

"Good enough," she said. "We have three other meats anyway, so we can do without the lamb."

"Exactly. I know the budget here is extensive," he said,

"but that doesn't mean it isn't a good idea sometimes to have one less meat a day."

"I was wondering about that," she said, "just to see if anybody noticed."

"Right," he said. "We could certainly do it for a few days and see what happens."

"I was wondering about doing it every second day or maybe once every three days," she said, "and putting in a vegetarian dish. Something even with a little protein that is heavy with vegetables."

"I like the idea," Gerard said. He was her number one assistant.

At that, she reached for the manifest Ricky handed her. She checked every item mentally against what recipes she needed it for with this week's menu plan and then signed the bottom. "Ricky, I think we'll need more lemons too," she said.

He nodded. "Okay," he said. "I'll add it to tomorrow's order."

Acknowledging the response, she turned, just as her phone rang. Pulling it out, she checked her Caller ID, seeing it was one her staff, then answered. "Stefan, how does it look today for you?"

"It is not good," he said, his soft voice apologetic. "Mom's having a bad day."

Ilse pinched the bridge of her nose with her free hand. "When can you come in?" she asked, not even believing that she was asking such a question. But Stefan was the only one looking after his mother, who had stage four breast cancer and was homebound. How did you even begin to ask somebody to come in when his life was falling apart like that?

"The hospice nurse will be coming this afternoon," he

said. "She'll be here for about an hour, and then I've got Rosy coming over to sit with her."

"So, you can come and help with dinner service then? That would work."

"The thing is, it can only work if everybody shows up as planned," he said hesitantly.

"I know," she said. "Otherwise, maybe tomorrow morning." After the call, she put away her phone and looked over to see the others quickly glancing away. "All right, you guys. What would you have me do?" she asked. "His mother is dying."

With that, she turned and walked out, heading to her office. She knew they would talk about it because no kitchen in any of the big companies would allow this behavior. But she wanted to be more than just a company and more than just another commercial kitchen. She wanted to show the heart and the face of what Hathaway House stood for in Dallas and worldwide. For the patients but for the staff as well.

She'd worked here for years and had seen how important it was to set the right tone. She had seen the success and the growth that came with it. She'd seen it in her own staff too, but this was a hard thing to let attendance slide because of the precedent it sent. And she knew that, as the top dog, she would step in to do Stefan's work. She didn't have a problem with that and had done it many times before and would do it many times in the future. But it was a whole different deal when it happened over and over again.

As she sat behind her desk with the paperwork to review, Ricky came in and handed off the signed forms that he'd stapled together with the others. "Okay," he said, "all these orders are clear."

She nodded, glanced to make sure it was all in order, and popped them into a folder.

"What will you work on now?" he asked, walking back to the doorway.

"Next week's menu," she said, standing up and walking over to the huge whiteboard that already had the days of the week lined out with spaces for the meals on each day.

"Do you want a hand?"

"I'll be fine," she said.

Ricky closed the door quietly behind him, and she stood here in silence for a long moment, wondering if and when any of these staff issues would ever change. She hoped soon for Stefan's sake, because his situation had to be just brutal. And her thoughts went from Stefan, with his dark hair and skinny body, to the dark-haired guy with the alabaster white skin and the frail body she had met earlier today. Keith, Robin's brother.

He obviously hadn't seen the sun in a year. His body had been beaten and torn first by the explosion and the associated physical and emotional trauma, then by all the surgical procedures trying to stitch him back together as well as possible. She had long been amazed at the versatility and the agility of the patients in this place but was stunned when she'd heard from Robin how many surgeries he'd had and what a mess his body still was at this point. She could only hope he would get through this.

She also hated the idea of him barely eating. *That's the chef in me*, she thought to herself. Going to bed on an empty stomach went against the grain, and she knew he'd sleep better with food, but only if it was something his stomach would tolerate. She quickly checked to see in her New Patient Notice if Keith had any dietary restrictions prescribed, and there were none. A lot of things upset his system because his stomach had taken some shrapnel too.

The last of that had been surgically removed, but it was a different story to get his gastrointestinal system settled again. She remembered that she had a good potato soup in the kitchen, and maybe that, with some big slabs of toasted French bread, might go down just fine. But not a whole lot of protein was in that.

Frowning, she walked back out to the kitchen, got a small pot, and quickly warmed up some of the soup, adding cheese and some chunks of ham. When she had a good thick broth, she put it into a bowl, toasted some French bread, and added a little plate she'd prepared with some sliced meat and cheese. With that done, she called Dennis in.

He came walking through, wearing his bright, cheerful smile as always. She pointed at the tray and said, "Keith just arrived today. He hasn't eaten, and he's saying no to food, but, when I was talking to him, I was thinking food might not be a bad idea."

Dennis immediately nodded. "That's Robin's brother, isn't it?"

She smiled and nodded. "Yeah, and he does not look happy to be here."

He looked at her in surprise.

She shrugged. "I don't think he's all that happy to be on the planet just now."

Understanding lit Dennis's face. They'd both been here for some time and had seen a lot of patients come and go, with some pretty serious physical and mental health issues. "I'll take this and see if I can get him to eat a little something," he said. He picked it up and walked out with the tray in his hand.

Gerard looked over at her. "Is he okay? The new guy?"

"First day. Traveling is brutal, and his surgical list is long enough for twenty-five people," she said, with a shake of her head. "The fact that he's even alive is pretty amazing, but his skin is pure white because he hasn't seen daylight or sunshine in probably a year or more." The others all winced at that. "We'll see if he eats."

She had just stepped back into her office when the phone rang with a call from Dani. "What's up?"

Chapter 2

"HEY," DANI SAID. "I just passed Dennis, and he said you were sending food down to Keith."

"Hoping to tempt him to eat a bit, yes," she said. "Problem?"

Dani chuckled. "Gosh no," she said. "I just wanted to thank you for being you."

Surprised, Ilse shrugged, even though she knew Dani couldn't see it. "It's all good. You know that."

"I know," Dani said, "but it's also why this place works," she said. "We come from the heart. That doesn't mean Keith's eating anything. It doesn't mean he'll even be in any condition to excel here," she said. "That was my concern with bringing in a family member, honestly. But we'll do our best by him regardless."

"Looks like a lot of people have done their best by him," Ilse said quietly. "Now he has to get to the point where he can offer that to himself."

"I know," Dani said, "and that's a mental shift that he'll have to figure out how to make. He's barely even recovered from the last of the surgeries, and I know his trip here was pretty brutal. But now that he's here, he can settle in and hopefully make some progress."

"Got it," she said. "I wouldn't mind keeping an eye out to see how he does," she said. "I know Robin will fill me in to a certain extent, but she said it would be okay if I walked down there to see if he needs anything later."

"If you want to do that, it's fine," Dani said in surprise. "But, given the number of relationships that happen around this place"—her humor slid into her voice—"you might want to watch out, just in case somebody's watching."

"You mean, the gossiping tongues?" Ilse asked drily. "I don't care who talks. That doesn't mean I'm listening."

"Got it," Dani said. "In that case, enjoy." And, with that, she hung up.

Ilse put down her phone, and, ignoring everything else around her, she picked up her marker and headed back to her meal planning calendar up on the wall, which kept track of what had been served over each season of the current year. For previous years, she had an Excel spreadsheet to keep track of those. Her whiteboard sat on an easel near the wall calendar, in case she was stumped on what to offer or just to check what may have been repeated too often or not often enough.

The menu was something she had to work on constantly. Never was an easy time to deal with it, though. And, from any given week, she carried certain favorites over as regulars. The food was always touted as being some of the best in facilities of this kind, and no way she would let any month, day, or week drop below that standard. It was just not in her to do any less today than she did yesterday. And, with that note, she started working on the next menu.

KEITH WAS DOZING in bed and shivering slightly when a knock on his door got his attention. He opened his eyes to see a huge male, wearing a big grin, walking in the door, carrying a tray. He put it down on the small swing table and moved it closer to the bed.

"Hi, I'm Dennis," he said. "Ilse sent this over for you."

He looked at the food, looked at Dennis, and said, "I'm pretty sure I told her that I didn't want anything to eat," he said with caution.

But Dennis studied him with a critical gaze. "And you're shivering," he said bluntly. "You need some hot soup, and we need to get you some warm blankets. You start eating. I'll take care of the other." With that, he was gone.

Now that he was more awake, Keith realized that he really was quite cold. The hot soup was a good idea; he hadn't really expected to get room service. It was a nice concept, but the thought that Ilse had sent it was what he struggled with. Still, he picked up the spoon and took a sip. Only partly admitting he was doing it for her.

Then he stopped, savoring the taste in his mouth before swallowing. Not only was it good and the flavors beautifully blended but it added a wonderfully warm and soothing element to his body. He picked up another spoonful chock-full of tender meat, and, before long, his soup was half gone.

He stared at his bowl, surprised. He almost never ate this much. And he noted a plate with meat and cheese was on the side too. At first, he wouldn't have any, but he picked up one and then a second piece. The next thing he knew, one of the big pieces of toast was gone, as was most of the meat and cheese.

By the time Dennis walked back into his room, Keith was pushing away the tray.

Dennis caught sight of it, looked at him, and said, "Wow, you were hungry." Quickly Dennis opened up the heated blanket and laid it across Keith's body.

Immediately he moaned. "Oh, God. Now I know how cold I was. I had no idea."

Dennis tucked him in, and the shivers started.

"You let those shivers work," Dennis ordered. "Let's get that body temperature back up again." He nodded at the tray. "You ate half of everything. Do you want any more?"

"I want to," he said, "but I'm scared of pushing my stomach."

"You know what? That's probably wise," he said. "Let's just call it quits with this amount right now, if that's okay with you."

Hesitating, Keith looked at it. "Let me have a few more bites of that soup." Struggling to keep the blanket tucked around his chest, he had another three or four spoonfuls until it was mostly gone. As the tray was about to go, he picked up the rest of the meat and cheese and said, "Okay, now I'm done."

"Good thing," Dennis said, "because the only thing you left was a half a piece of bread."

He smiled, sank back into the covers. "Man, I don't know where you got this heated blanket from, but, God, it's exactly what I needed."

"Yeah, we all need them sometimes," he said. "Now hopefully you'll get some sleep tonight. That must have been a rough trip getting here."

"Yeah, it was pretty painful. Right now, I'm mostly just cold," he said.

"Of course you are. Your body has been through a lot. Now rest. That's what you need."

He nodded and sank farther under the covers, slowly munching the last of the meat and cheese. By the time that was gone, his eyelids drifted closed. He wasn't sure how Ilse had known what he wanted to eat, but it was a perfect choice, and he appreciated it.

As soon as he got the chance, he would tell her. Later. Anything that required movement right now was way too much to contemplate. He closed his eyes, and, within minutes, he fell asleep.

Chapter 3

WHEN ILSE WALKED from her on-site apartment into the center in the wee hours of the morning, she took a long, deep breath. She loved the place when it was quiet and almost empty. It was five o'clock in the morning. She didn't always come in at this hour, but she had woken up and couldn't get back to sleep, so she figured she'd get an early start on breakfast. She knew that some of her crew would already be here, but she had her own keys to get in and out.

Nobody manned the front desk yet, but nurses would be on, orderlies around, and, of course, her kitchen staff filtering in. She walked the long hallway where a light shone through a door partially open. She frowned at the idea that she wasn't the only one awake a little too early.

"Good morning," she called out softly as she walked by. The voice that called back was one she recognized. Stopping, she turned around, walked back, and poked her head in the door. "What are you doing awake so early?" she asked Keith.

He looked at her in surprise. "I guess you're up early, being a chef and all, huh?"

"I could work nine to five," she said, "but I'd much rather work early."

"Aren't you here for all the meals?"

"Sometimes," she said. "Sometimes I take a few hours off

in the afternoon. It all depends on what I'm cooking."

"And I guess it also depends on whether you have a decent staff or not," he said with a smile.

"I have a very decent staff," she said. "I wouldn't have it any other way. But it's hard to let go of control on something like that."

He nodded.

As he shifted uneasily in his bed, she watched him, knowing he was already in pain. "So, let me guess. The pain is getting to you, and you can't go back to sleep."

He shrugged. "Seems like something I just live with these days."

"I don't think you have to do that here," she said. "The hot tub and the pool might be something you could use."

"And that might help too," he said. "I don't know. I hate to ask anybody to give me a hand getting there."

"Asking for help is hard," she said, "but it's also pretty necessary."

He just smiled but didn't say any more.

"So, I'll go make a fresh pot of coffee," she said, wagging her eyebrows at him. "You interested?" She watched the surprise light up his dark eyes, and, in spite of himself, he smiled and nodded slowly.

"That would be awesome," he said. "And thank you for dinner last night. That soup was delicious."

She smacked the doorjamb as she walked back out again. "See you in a few." She headed down to her kitchen. Stepping inside her gleaming domain, she smiled. She didn't know what she would do if she ever came in to find it completely destroyed or something because this was her space. This was where she belonged. It was her home, and a home she wanted spick-and-span and in perfect order at all times.

Gerard was already in. She rolled her eyes at him. "What are you up to?"

"You gave me free license to make pasta," he said with a big grin. "So, here I am, making pasta."

As she surveyed the kitchen, he had several counters full of rectangles of dough already laid out to be cut. "You're hand cutting it?"

He nodded. "After you put on coffee," he said with an encouraging smile. "We've been waiting for you to come in."

"And why would you do that?" she asked.

"Because you are about to turn on the espresso machine," he said with a laugh. "We just made regular drip coffee, and we already drank it."

"Well, I do like my espresso in the morning," she said comfortably. "But I'll put on a pot of drip too." And that's what she did.

By the time she walked over with a cup for Gerard and for herself, he already had most of the dough cut and was laying everything onto a mobile unit of strings and long poles to roll in the backroom to dry.

"They won't dry very much if we use them today," she warned him.

"I know," he said. "They'll dry just enough."

She laughed and gave him a hand.

By the time all the noodles were hung, he looked remarkably proud of himself. She had to admit they looked lovely. "Maybe I'll take a picture of that and post it on the website," she said. "We'll see how many people choose fresh pasta today." Pulling out her phone, she took several shots, including some with Gerard beside his work. "Now, let's get our coffee." And then she remembered her promise. "Oh, but I have to deliver a cup first."

He looked at her in surprise.

"One of the patients is awake," she said. "I met him yesterday, and, when I walked past his room, I saw his light was on, so I called out a good morning and stopped for a minute."

Gerard nodded. "Potato-soup dude?"

"Yeah, exactly. Potato-soup dude," she said, laughing. "Good thing I sent it up. He ate 99 percent of it."

"Wow," Gerard said. "We should be doing more of that, shouldn't we? You know? Checking out the patients ourselves to make sure they're getting what they need from us."

"Well, I'm pretty sure Dani has all that taken care of, but I do think it would be a good idea every once in a while for us to spend some time visiting with the patients, to see just what they'd like to eat."

"I think the last time we did that," he said, "we had menu ideas for six months."

"Considering that I struggled with the menu board just yesterday," she said, "that's not a bad idea." She walked over and poured a cup of drip coffee, put it on a small tray with milk, sugar, and a spoon, just in case. "I'll be back in a few minutes."

"I'll be here," he said.

Tray in hand, she headed back down the hallway, wondering whether Keith would be sleeping by now or not. She walked to the doorway, finding it was still open, the light still on. She poked her head through and saw he was just lying there, his eyes barely closed. "I don't want to wake you," she said quietly, "but the coffee's here."

He smiled. "I'm not asleep, just resting. Boy, that coffee sure smells good."

She walked in and set the tray on a small table, unloading the contents. "I didn't know how you like your coffee, so I brought milk and sugar, just in case."

"Normally nothing," he said. "Definitely not sugar but sometimes a little cream, depending on how strong it is."

She added a little milk and passed him the coffee cup. "I'm not sure if you're up for pasta or not, but check this out." She held up her phone to show him a picture. "One of my guys just finished making these."

He looked at it in surprise. "Fresh noodles?"

She nodded.

"I'll have pasta," he said. "Lunch or dinner?"

"We might split it and do both," she said with a frown. "Or we might leave half the noodles to dry and have them in a couple days."

"Well, whatever you do, save me a little bit," he said. "I can't get much down, but I would really enjoy some fresh pasta."

"Have you ever had it?" she asked.

"Oh, yeah. My mother used to make it," he said with a smile.

"In that case, we better tell Robin it's available too," she said.

He laughed at that. "Yeah, I don't think she'd like it if I got special treatment andshe got left out."

"Well, you are a patient, after all," she said, as she walked back over to the door. "Now you better drink your coffee, then get a little more sleep if you can. Otherwise, wake up and enjoy the day."

He lifted the cup and took a tiny sip, then leaned back with a blissful sigh.

Still chuckling, she headed down the hallway.

As soon as she walked in the kitchen, Gerard looked at her and smiled. "Now that's an interesting look on your face."

"Why is that?" she asked, not really understanding what was on his mind. But, then again, it was Gerard after all.

"You like him," he said.

She looked at him in surprise. "What's not to like?" she said. "The guy has survived over thirty surgeries. I'd like anybody who was still finding a way forward after being as patchworked and pieced-together as he is. If nothing else, I like his grit."

"And that's something you've always admired, isn't it?"

"Yes," she said. "I admire anybody who deals with adversity and still gets up."

"Because you have done so too," he said with a nod.

She rolled her eyes at him. "Don't you have something better to do?"

"Better than teasing you? No," he said with a laugh. "But I am sitting here, wondering what I want to do with the pasta. I made a lot."

"I was wondering, as I walked back down, about using half of it today and letting the other half dry out a couple days to be used later."

"You know something? That's not a bad idea. I wouldn't be at all unhappy to try some more fresh pasta next week—or maybe some raviolis."

"I'm up for that too," she said. "I think I'll make some fresh bread this morning. Maybe a double-baked Swiss loaf." Putting down her cup, she grabbed a big bowl and starting measuring ingredients.

"I still don't understand how you can keep all those recipes in your head," he said, as he watched her.

She smiled, adding the yeast and just enough warm water, plus a dab of sugar, to proof before measuring the flour, and she had a ball of dough quickly mixed up. She tossed it from the bowl onto the marble counter and kneaded it. "I've probably got enough here for what, six loaves?" She thought about it and then took a knife, cut it into multiple long loaves, and said, "It's not very much for breakfast. I guess what I probably should have done was double that."

"Not necessarily," he said. "We always have so much variety at breakfast that not everybody even wants bread."

She nodded. "Then maybe we'll add some raisins and butter to this loaf."

He immediately snatched up another one and said, "Let's have cranberries and walnuts in this one."

Together, the two of them laughed as they created several breakfast rolls, instead of the double-baked Swiss bread she had started with. The other breads still used the same basic foundation recipe, but she could do so much more with these. By the time they finished adding lemon peel and extra butter to the last one, they had all six stretched out to rise, each a good two feet long.

Other staff members were coming in, and two were in the back, already cooking the bacon for breakfast. The ham would go on next; then the sausages would work their way onto the big grill. Pancakes still had to be done. Then, of course, the eggs and all the extras.

Dennis walked in just then, following his nose, smelling the coffee. "Wow. Every time you have espresso," he said, "it's like a hit to my heart, and it makes me smile."

"It's a weird way of smiling," she said.

He walked past the open storeroom, stopped, and then whistled. "Man, I hope that's for lunch," he said. "I sure want some."

"See?" Gerard said. "Everybody wants fresh pasta."

She rolled her eyes.

"Ask her who she delivered coffee to this morning," Gerard said, nudging Dennis.

He turned and looked at her in surprise. "You delivered coffee?"

At his tone, she fisted her hands on her hips. "And what if I did?"

He immediately held up his hands to ward off any comments and stepped back in mock terror.

She just sighed. "What is it about guys and gals?"

"Well, that's what we're trying to figure out," Gerard said, "because you delivered coffee to a guy, and you came back with a special smile on your face."

She groaned. "Oh, my God, you two. The guy just got here, and he's had a raw deal. He was awake, so I offered him coffee. End of subject." But she watched Gerard and Dennis nudge each other, laughing like schoolboys. "Maybe you two would want to get some work done, huh? Everything ready for breakfast?" she asked, heading over to the latest arrival. "Need you to step up on the juices, if you don't mind, and make sure the coolers are stocked."

Dennis called over to her, "I just came in to get a dozen juice bottles, but I'll fill the big cooler instead, and we've got to get the coffee going. Are people out there now?"

"Yeah, I've got six. I did a small pot for them and then refilled it, but we'll have a bunch more now, so let's get the big coffeemakers going."

And with the hustle-and-bustle happening in the kitchen with breakfast preparation, before long the rush was to get everything out on time and then, of course, to feed everybody. She stepped in the back of the cafeteria line and kept watch to make sure there was enough and that everything went smoothly. It was weird how one day the big run was on eggs, the next day no sausage would be left, then a few days would go by, and it seemed like nobody was even hungry at all, but then not a slice of bacon was left in the building.

By the time breakfast was over, everybody was happy and settled, the dishes were well in hand, if not done, and they were already prepping for lunch. She had several roasts in the oven, and she left Gerard to deal with the pasta. She would do up a huge roasted veggie platter, so the preparation was underway for that.

"I want something with fish," she said to one of her guys. "What can we do that we haven't done lately?"

"How about we roll it up in parmesan and add a bit of a lemon zest to it."

She looked at him in surprise. Sammy hadn't been with her very long, but he had some really good ideas. "You know how to do it?"

He looked at her in surprise and then slowly nodded.

"Good, you're it," she said. When he hesitated, she looked at him and said, "Questions?"

"Yeah," he said, "I get that I'm it, but I don't know how much to do."

She thought about that for a moment and said, "Let's do twenty pounds." She walked with him into the freezer, and they pulled out fillets. By the time she had what she thought was a perfect amount, and they had them laid out on cookie sheets to thaw properly, he was already preparing the breading for them.

"Remember. Not too strong," she cautioned. "Lots of touchy tummies around here."

"I know," he said, "but it's a really good recipe."

"Sounds like it," she said, "and we also have to make sure that, when we fry them up, it's not greasy."

He hesitated before he said, "We could do it in the oven. That would be faster."

"Wouldn't necessarily be as tasty though, correct?"

He grinned with relief. "No, that's exactly it."

"Well, we have the fryers," she said. "We'll have to set the temperature for fish, not for french fries, and then they'll have to be babied."

"I got it," he said.

She watched him as he straightened his shoulders and stood a little taller. She nodded. "You do. So let's see what you've got."

With that, he grinned and turned back to his dish.

She wandered over to check on the roasted veggies. It was amazing just how much they shrunk down by the time they went through the oven, so, to end up with a great big roasting pan full of roasted vegetables, plus another full roasting pan for backup, meant that she would have to cook a good forty pounds of the raw veggies. She watched as they brought out the fresh parsnips. "Wow," she said, reaching for a big long white one. "I haven't seen anything this size for quite a few months."

"They look really good," Jose said, as he picked up his chopping knife and started whacking away at them.

She watched the veggie piles build up really fast. Then she grabbed the olive oil and drizzled it over them, throwing in rock salt and taking up her big pepper grinder. By the time all of the veggies were prepped, seasoned, and into great big roasting pans, all the ovens were ready, and everything went in.

She walked over and turned the air conditioner up a little bit. By the time the ovens were running at four hundred degrees, the kitchens got very hot. She didn't mind hot, but she didn't want it getting so hot that they all got tired and too fatigued. Lots left to do.

"Where are the desserts?" she called over to the far side of kitchen, where the sweet endings to a meal were being made. They had the usual things, like pudding, an institute staple. But also black forest cake, cardamom cake, and three pies, and it looked like Sandy was making some miniature crumbles. "Are you baking those?"

"No," she said, "these aren't custards though. They are cream based."

"Interesting," she said. She reached over with a spoon, snagged up a little taste, and nodded. "It's a bit bland. Maybe a tad more vanilla."

Obediently Sandy picked up the vanilla, added a bit more, and mixed it in, then tasted it herself. "Yeah, you're right." And she went back to work, creating these parfaits. What Ilse thought was crumble on the top was just spices.

With all of that on the go, she headed over to check on the basics, like bread, muffins, and buns that were done on another side of the kitchen. They had so many ovens going on a regular basis here that something was always cooking. As she watched, a whole mess of dinner buns came out of the oven. She smiled at the fresh yeast smell. "Do you have anything else to go in these ovens?" she asked Bert.

"These buns are done," he said. "I don't have anything else to go in for"—he checked his watch—"about forty-two minutes."

"Oh, good," she said, as she adjusted the temperature. "I've got six loaves to go in."

They quickly got those in; they only took fifteen minutes. Once they were done, she brought them out, quickly sliced them, and set them on the counter. Most of the breakfast foods were done, but still a lot of people came through looking for something light. As soon as they smelled the fresh bread, it disappeared quickly, and, with such a commotion at the cafeteria line, many of the people sitting down got up and came back for some.

By the time she had a chance to turn around and to check the cafeteria line, all the loaves were gone, and just one tiny piece sat off to one side. She quickly snagged it up, stacked up all the pans the bread had been on, and brought them back in empty.

The guys looked at her, then looked at the pans. One shook his head. "Those guys are pigs."

She laughed. "That they are, but they sure enjoyed it. One piece is left." She handed it to Gerard.

He snagged it, took a bite, and a blissful smile crossed his face.

"Don't tell me that's your special bread you made this morning," Sandy said sorrowfully.

"It is," Ilse said. "Nothing's left." She pointed at all the empty serving dishes. "It's all gone."

Sandy shook her head. "Next time make twice as much."

Laughing, Ilse said, "It wasn't even what I intended to make."

"That's what you said last time too," Gerard said. "It's hardly fair when you don't even intend to make something like this, and it turns out absolutely divine."

"Well, maybe I'll have to do something else tomorrow," she said. "I just like to have dough in my hands."

"Feel free," Sandy said, "whatever you want to make."

"I might make a nut braid or something or other for dessert tonight," Ilse said. "I'll have to think about it."

The trouble was that, even as she was thinking, her hands were working. Or at least wanting to work. She snagged up another big bowl, started measuring in flour, added two pounds of chopped butter, then walked over and grabbed ice water from the fridge. She added more salt and more yeast, while everybody surreptitiously watched her. She ignored them.

She had recipes in her head from her grandmother and her mother, and this was an old favorite. It was super-superlight and fluffy, and, with the dough already mixed up, she chopped more butter in until it was flaky and almost too soft. Then she sprinkled out a bit of flour on the marble countertop, laid the dough there, and kneaded it gently. Then she kneaded more butter into it. By the time she was done, she had this huge ball of soft butter dough.

"What will you do with that?" Gerard asked, standing at her side. He was boiling fresh pasta noodles and making a bacon and cream sauce beside her. Leftover bacon from breakfast had him tweaking his original cream sauce idea for the pasta, so he used all the bacon for that.

She rolled out the dough quickly, then made up a brown sugar, walnut, and raisin mixture, placing a thick, heavy bead of it down the center. She then braided over the top slices that she had cut, closing it up on either end, leaving her with a great big soft buttery braid. She put it on the baking sheet, let it rise for twenty minutes, and, when that was done, popped it into one of the ovens that was about the right temperature.

"Why is it you never seem to worry about temperatures?" Sandy asked thoughtfully. "Everybody is really specific about being so long at a certain temperature."

"There's optimum, yes," she said, not really paying attention. "The trouble is, not every oven is the same. You have to understand what your oven can do, and then you have to figure out what your leeway is on each item."

She waited twenty minutes. When she pulled it out, everybody walked over to take a look. It had risen and flaked, so now the walnut brown sugar center was gooey, inside this very buttery dough. Everybody just looked at her, and she laughed. "It's for lunch."

"I thought you'd make something for dinner," he said.

"I was, and then I decided to do this." She cut it into thin strips and carefully laid it on two separate plates so that it could be taken out for dessert at lunchtime. She left several slices in the pan and said, "But now it's coffee time." Everybody immediately grabbed one.

Gerard pushed his over toward her. "Don't you want a bite?"

She looked at it, hesitated, "Maybe a bite," she said. With her second cup of coffee, she took a bite of his, then headed to her office. She got to play in the kitchen a lot, but that didn't change or take away from the fact that she had a ton of paperwork to do as well.

As soon as she sat down, she realized she probably should have taken a little piece of that to Keith. She walked back out, saw one piece still left there, and asked, "Is this mine?"

Nearly in unison they all said, "Yes."

She immediately put it on a small plate and walked out. She heard Gerard say, "So much for her eating it. You want to take bets on where she's going?"

She sighed, knowing that just being friendly to a patient

was causing her to be the butt of the gossip. She knew they meant it only in the best of ways, but it was still kind of irritating. She walked down the hallway to see one of the doctors stepping out of Keith's room. He smiled at her, turned, and went the opposite direction. She stepped inside his room. "I know that you've got nothing but traffic coming and going here," she said, "but I thought I'd bring you this." She placed it on the small tray next to his bed.

He looked at it in surprise. "Wow, I don't even know what that is."

"I'm not sure I have a name for it either," she said. "It's one of my grandmother's favorites."

Picking it up, he took a bite and sank back onto his bed. "My God," he said, barely able to speak. "This is delicious."

"Good," she said. "I did one huge loaf, which is cooling now, in order to go out for lunch."

"Man, I'll get so fat while I'm here," he muttered.

"You could stand to put on some pounds," she said, laughing. "You're skin and bones."

He nodded. "The surgeries haven't been too easy on me."

"No, but that's done and gone. It's a new day." She looked at her watch and said, "I better get back. Lunch service will start here soon."

"I don't even know if I'm supposed to go to the lunchroom," he said.

She looked at him in surprise. "You've got a tablet there. Call Dani and ask her."

He looked at it in surprise and asked, "Can I do that?"

"Send her a message." She walked back over, brought the tablet out of Sleep mode, and said, "Here. Dani's right there, so you can send her a message." She tapped the icon, brought up the text box, and said, "Go for it."

While she watched, he quickly typed in a message, asking if he was supposed to make it to lunch on his own. But, instead of getting a response, they heard footsteps coming down the hallway.

"Uh-oh," Ilse said. "Time for me to leave."

"Did you get me in trouble?" he growled in a mocking voice.

"Nope," she said. "I think it was probably easier for her to explain in person than message you back."

"Exactly," Dani said, as she walked into his room. "Your sister is taking you to lunch."

"Oh," he said in delight. "I hadn't even considered that."

"You're not used to having your sister around, are you?"

He stopped, then shook his head. "Not for a long time."

IT *HAD* BEEN a long time. Keith didn't quite know how to explain it, but, with him in the military and her at the university full-time, they didn't have a whole lot of opportunity to spend time together. But he could see from their faces that they understood. He had noticed that, around here, every time he tried to explain something, they'd already gotten it. Somehow they understood.

It was disconcerting, but he remembered seeing a TV show once, where a woman said that, when people got her jokes, she felt that she had found her people and was happy because now she had people who understood her. Maybe that's what this was all about for him. Maybe he had found his people here. It was a weird feeling, like a sense of belonging that he hadn't expected to feel again. Being in the navy, and especially being a SEAL, he had experienced the same feeling of brotherhood, of belonging, but, once he was injured and separated from the team, knowing he could never go back there, he also felt that sense of being left behind. Something he didn't ever want to feel again.

But now he was here and wondering if maybe these were his people in a sense. Just then another set of footsteps walked down the hallway. He looked up to see that Ilse had left, and Dani remained.

Looking at him, Dani asked, "How are you holding up?" She looked at the dessert in his hand. "Wow, did she deliver that for you?"

"Yes," he said, popping the last bite into his mouth. "She did. But apparently there's more for lunch, which is in about an hour, I understand." Just then his sister poked her head around the corner.

"Hey, bro. I meant to tell you that I will go down to lunch with you, if you're okay with that."

He laughed. "I think you're the last one to tell me," he said, "but thanks. That sounds good."

She looked surprised at his tone and also pleased.

That made him realize just how much of a grouch and a generally miserable human being he'd been over the last year or so. He needed to make it up to his sister, but first he had to make it up to himself. Maybe, just maybe, by being here, he could make some progress in that area too.

Chapter 4

A COUPLE DAYS later, Ilse walked up the center stairs in the morning and walked down the hallway. She could feel herself already edging toward Keith's room, looking to see if he was awake. And, sure enough, once again the light was on. She poked her head around the corner to see him waiting, almost expectantly. She smiled. "I think this is a bad habit."

He gave her a sheepish smile. "Believe me. I'm not trying to be awake when you arrive. I would love to sleep late."

"I know," she said sadly. "How have your first few days here been?"

"Good," he said, "but we haven't really done anything yet. Just lots of testing." He shuffled restlessly in the bed, then shut his eyes.

"You'll go back to sleep?"

"It hasn't happened yet," he said, "but I guess it's possible."

"So, no coffee?"

His eyes popped opened. "Definitely coffee," he said warmly. "I just feel bad having you deliver it all the time."

"My legs are working," she said, "and they're young and healthy, so really no reason I can't bring a coffee back." And, with that, she gave him a small finger wave and walked on past.

She had been pretty busy, partly because recently they'd been shorted on several orders. When a big mix-up on another order had her wondering what kind of craziness was going on in her world, she'd finally pulled Ricky aside and sat him down to ask him what was going on.

Then she found out that he had been really distracted because his daughter had seen a specialist, and she might have leukemia. Her heart had gone out to him immediately, as she became aware that she now had two of her staff dealing with major health issues in their family. "Okay, but I'll take over the ordering for now," she said. "These last few days have been a mess."

He winced and nodded. "Do I still have a job?"

"Of course you do," she said warmly. "I understand you are distracted. Who wouldn't be? But I can't have you doing a job with such big ramifications when a mistake gets made." She laughed and tried to put him at ease.

He nodded. "I was trying to get it right, then, after finding a mistake, I'd panic. In the course of trying to fix it, half the time I just made it worse. Way worse."

She looked down at his notes that had been scratched out and written over and scratched off again, and the order forms looked a bit like a kid's messy homework paper.

She nodded and said, "You need time to clear your head, so you can do whatever needs to be done around here that doesn't require this stuff." She held out the papers. "Let me see it."

He handed her the clipboard with a new ordering sheet in front.

"Do you have any idea what we need?"

He stared at her, then sighed. "Not really."

She nodded. "Okay, let's go then. The two of us can

walk through and see what we need. Grab the old sheets so we can see what we ordered over the last couple weeks."

She already knew that she needed fresh mushrooms and green peas. She needed another shipment of flour. Making notes as they walked, the two of them went through the stock slowly and carefully. Not like an inventory but making a list of what they would need going forward. When that was finally done, she'd missed her coffee and realized she hadn't delivered any to Keith either. But she did have her order sheets done.

She quickly faxed in one of them that she needed today, hoping it wasn't too late, then sent the other two off for tomorrow's deliveries. With the lists in her hand, she walked over and readjusted the week's menu based on the different ingredients they were bringing in now.

When she turned around, Ricky just stood there, staring off into space. She gave him a gentle shake on the shoulder. "Go home. If your family needs you, that's where you should be."

He looked at her in surprise.

She shrugged and said, "We can handle this while you look after your daughter. Just go."

He didn't waste any time and quickly grabbed his jacket and was gone.

Gerard looked over at her, asking, "What was that all about?"

"He's a mess right now," she said, explaining about his daughter going in for leukemia testing. At that news, everybody winced.

"Well, that explains the orders for the last few days."

"Yes, I'm just sorry he didn't tell us before we ended up with whatever it is. Twenty-four extra gallons of milk?" She shook her head at that. "We need ways to use it, people."

"Puddings," one of them said immediately.

"Cream soups," another one said.

"Good. Keep those ideas coming," she said. "We've got a seven-day window for the 'best before' dates, so let's book out something every day that'll use up what we have. Twenty-four/seven. Dividing that up, it looks like we'll need to use an extra three gallons a day."

They nodded and turned back to the work they each were doing.

She walked over, finding the coffee was once again gone, and put on a fresh pot. As soon as it had dripped, she poured herself one and another for Keith, even though it was two hours late. She slipped out of the kitchen and headed toward his room.

When she walked inside, he was sitting up and looking a little worse for the wear. He had a sheet thrown across his leg, but the other leg she could see was purple and black. She stopped and winced. "Man, I hope the other one doesn't look quite so bad."

He stared down at the puffy-looking mess. "It does, unfortunately. Maybe worse actually."

"Can you walk at all?"

"I can," he said, "but not very far, not very fast, and not very long."

"Still, being ambulatory is huge," she said, putting the coffee down. "Sorry, things got crazy in the kitchen."

He looked at the coffee in surprise. "I'd forgotten. I fell asleep and didn't remember when I woke up that no cold coffee waited here for me."

She grinned at that. "In that case, it's a good thing that I got sidetracked." Just like that, she turned to leave again.

"Wait," he called out.

She turned to look at him. "What's up?" She saw him hesitate and then shrug.

"Nothing really, but thanks for the coffee."

Knowing he was trying to say something else but wouldn't now, she wished she had given him an opportunity to speak before she left. Aware that the moment was lost, she shrugged and said, "You're welcome." And, with that, she headed back to the kitchen.

KEITH DIDN'T EVEN know what he should say. She was going out of her way every day to say hi first thing in the morning, to ask him about coffee, and then she came by and brought him one. He wasn't used to this special attention, certainly not from a chef in a place like this. She was also super friendly and approachable. He always figured chefs were these six-foot-tall men with massive chests and beer guts, hacking out orders like a command center in a big kitchen. She was the complete antithesis to who he thought would run a kitchen here.

But, from the food that he had tasted, it was absolutely exquisite. And lots of it, which was not that easy to do. Institutional food was well-known for being bland, overcooked, and completely tasteless. But not here. Not here at all. Yet another bonus of his visit. But, like he'd said to her, so far nothing was happening. It was just testing. And that was frustrating.

He slid off the edge of the bed, grabbed his crutches, and supported himself on the aluminum "sticks" while he tried to stand. He had told her that he could walk, and he could—

but only in an emergency. One step, two steps. In the meantime, getting from point A to point B without crutches was a major trauma to his system. The right leg still dragged more than he would like. But he managed to make it to the bathroom, and, after using the facilities, he wondered about a quick shower, then decided to go for it, regardless of whether it was the thing to do or not. Of course his shower was equipped with all the bars and seats needed for people like him.

He turned on the hot water and made his way under the heavy stream and just sat here, letting the heat beat down on his head and body. He stared down his body, at the one leg that she'd seen, studying it, as if with her eyes. He'd become so used to the scars that crisscrossed his body that the purple welts and the new tissue never looked the same as the old tissue.

He was like a Frankenstein put back together again. Modern medicine had done a heck of a job, but it hadn't left him in very pretty shape.

By the time he was done with his shower and got dressed and back to his bed, he was shaking. He swore lightly.

Just then a man spoke around the corner. "That doesn't sound good."

Keith glared at the open door. "It's not bad though," he said to Shane.

Shane walked in, frowning at him. "What exhausted you this morning?"

"I just had a shower," he said.

Shane looked at him in surprise. "Did you get there under your own steam?"

He nodded.

"Did you have the shower on your own?"

He nodded again.

"Did you get back here and get dressed on your own?"

At that, he nodded once more.

"Then I sure wouldn't be too upset with that much effort on your own," Shane said with a big smile. "I'm thrilled to know you have that much independence."

He stared at him in surprise. "Yeah, but, I mean, I'm exhausted," he said. "I could barely even make it back."

"*Barely* is a mind-set," Shane announced. "The thing to remember is you *did* make it. Now how about some breakfast?"

"I was thinking about it, but I'm pretty tired now," he admitted.

"No problem," Shane said. He grabbed the wheelchair, pulled it around, and said, "Let's use this."

He looked at it, then at Shane, and said, "I generally don't go out in public in a wheelchair."

"Hathaway House is not *public*," he said. "This is home, so hop in."

Shane was just one of those guys who was really hard to ignore or to argue with. The wheelchair sat in front of Keith, one of those specters of his current life that he hated, but no give was in Shane's voice or in the look on his face. He'd already slid the wheelchair his way, and Shane reached out and grabbed Keith's arm.

"Easy," he said. "If you slide down, take one step forward. Then we can twist you and drop you into the seat."

And that's what they did. And even though Keith was tall, once he was in a wheelchair, he felt like a child. "I hate these things," he muttered.

"Of course you do," he said, "because, to you, it's a backward step. What you're forgetting is to be grateful for the fact that you have the option of a wheelchair, so you can get breakfast without collapsing halfway there."

With Shane pushing, giving Keith zero option on direction, he was pushed out of the room, down the hallway toward the cafeteria. He looked around and said, "Aren't many people in wheelchairs here."

"On any given day," Shane said, "there'll be dozens, and it can change from morning to afternoon. If you've had your PT workout, and you can't make it back, the wheelchair is an easy option."

"Is that what happens to a lot of guys?" he asked. Because, in his experience, it hadn't happened to him yet.

"All the time," Shane said cheerfully. "All the time."

"So it'll get harder here than it's been so far?" A startled breath escaped from Shane behind him, so Keith twisted, wincing as he did so. He stared up at the physiotherapist.

"You haven't seen anything yet," Shane said quietly. "And, when the time comes, you'll remember this conversation and wish you hadn't brought it up."

"That bad?"

"That bad," Shane said, and he gave him a flat stare. "We'll tailor it to what you can do, but what you think you can do is always different than what I know you can do."

Chapter 5

THE PATTERN CONTINUED for the next few days. Ilse would say hi to him in the morning, if he was awake, then bring him coffee if she could. She would try to greet him at lunch, even though she was normally behind-the-scenes. Even Dennis commented on it.

"Wow, there must be something special about him that's dragged you out of your kitchen."

"I don't know what it is," she said quietly. "After I saw his leg, the hamburger that is left of it,"—she shook her head—"I don't think I could have done what he's done."

Dennis nodded slowly. "A lot of guys here are like that," he said. "I guess this is just the first time you've come in contact with one on a personal level."

"I don't think I could do it too often," she said, staring at the long queue forming out front at the dessert and coffee station. "The fact that he's still even functional, after so many surgeries, just blows me away. I understand the depression and the lack of vitality. I don't even think it's so much of a mental state for him as much as his body is still recovering from everything that's been done to him."

"Well, I know that you put a smile on his face," Dennis said, "so, for that, we're all grateful. What is it about him that gets to you?"

They kept their voices low because they were still out

front, behind the cafeteria line. She leaned against the back counter with Dennis beside her, as they watched the full cafeteria eating happily as the line began dissipating around the desserts.

"I'm not sure," she said, then shook her head. "Just something about him that hits at a different level for me."

"Well, he is certainly an interesting new addition," Dennis said. "He's got grit, which is a good thing, because he's got a long, hard journey ahead of him."

She looked at him sharply. "Will it be as bad as the journey he's already left behind?"

At that, he looked at her in surprise. "You know what? I'm not sure that it is," he said. "Chances are the worst is behind him. He'll work hard here for every inch of progress, but he will see the gains this time. The thing about all his surgeries is that he had to recover just so he could go back and get cut again. Although they might have done a really great job, the gains aren't necessarily anything he can really see or feel because his body must still be such a mess. The next six months for him will be huge."

"I wonder how far he can go?"

"I mentioned that to Shane a few days ago, and he said nothing was holding Keith back, now that the last of the surgeries were completed. He has a lot of work ahead of him, but there was every reason to think that he could lead a fully functioning life again after this."

"Well, that's a relief," she said. "I think he's almost stuck in that zone where he doesn't see progress, doesn't think there'll be any, and doesn't know why anybody bothers anymore."

"Yes, I see that too," Dennis said. "There's very little in the way of laughter or even smiles in his world."

"I don't think there has been for a long time."

"I'm glad his sister brought him here," Dennis said. "Robin has had a lot to do with any smiles we do see."

"But someone shouldn't have to *try* to smile," she said sadly. "Do you think his world has beaten him up so much that smiles are something he has to force out? That's just sad."

"You may find that just being around him will lighten him up a little bit, and he'll have more reasons to smile. The trip here couldn't have been easy, and the adjustments here aren't easy either. Just knowing you are taking a few minutes to visit with him in the morning helps too, I think."

"Does everybody know about that?" she asked with a sense of humor. "I'm not even sure why I started it, but now it feels like I can't stop it."

"Do you want to stop those visits with Keith?"

As always, Dennis had a zinger of a question, and he went for the jugular with it. She crossed her arms over her chest while she thought about it because a question like that deserved the time for a real answer and not just a flippant comeback. "Stop? No, I don't think I do," she said. "The place is so quiet in the morning. It's fresh and feels renewed or something. It's hard to explain, but, when I come in each morning, it feels like all things are possible. And when I stop and see that his light is on and that he's awake, it's just the two of us in the foggy world all around us, and something's special about that." She gave a quick nod. "The fact that sometimes he's awake, and sometimes he's not, that sometimes I remember his coffee, and sometimes I forget, keeps it changing." She laughed. "It's not a routine really. It's more like just a connection that we get to make and then move on."

"Or not move on," Dennis said, with an arched eyebrow.

She laughed again. "No, it's nothing like that."

"Too bad," he said. "You haven't had a relationship in years."

"Keeping track of my love life now?" she teased. "Remember though, if you do that to me, I get to do it back."

He rolled his eyes at her. "That's the thing. Nobody can hide from anybody in this place."

"Maybe that's okay too," she said, "because, if you know the shields won't work, why put them up in the first place? And we all spend way too much time building those walls against the rest of the world. I hide in my kitchen, and it makes perfect sense to me, but other people think it's terrible."

"But most people don't think about it that way," he said. "They just batten down the hatches even tighter, hoping that nobody will notice that they've got a wall up."

"And very often they don't," she said sadly, "because everybody else's walls are even higher."

"This place does something to you," Dennis said. "It opens our eyes and our hearts."

She nodded.

Just then one of the patients called out to him. He hopped over to him. "What can I get for you, sir?"

She watched as Dennis, with that big affable smile of his, served a patient. She relaxed here and watched as Dennis interacted with the next few who came by. Something was special about Dennis too. She wished he could find a partner in life, particularly after they'd seen so many relationships come through this place. But, much like her, he hadn't had the time, the opportunity, or just that right connection yet.

As she was about to head back into the kitchen, she saw Shane pushing a wheelchair. From where she was, she could see that it was Keith. For whatever reason, realizing he was in a wheelchair made his condition all that much worse. He'd said he was ambulatory, but she had yet to see him walking—with crutches or without. To see him in a wheelchair seemed like a step back. But he also looked worn out, and she knew he hadn't even started whatever physical therapy sessions they had in store for him here. She could only wish that he paced himself over the next few weeks because, no matter how bad today was, tomorrow would be a whole lot worse.

THE VISIT TO the cafeteria had been fine, and, after that, he'd gone on his own for dinner and then again for lunch and dinner the next day. But, on Friday, Shane walked into his room and asked, "You ready to get to work?"

"Well, I wish," he said, "but it doesn't seem like you guys have any work for me to do."

Shane chuckled. "That's all right. We'll get started today." He looked at him and said, "Shorts and a T-shirt."

"My leg is pretty ugly. It might scare the nurses." But he grabbed the crutches and went across to the drawers, where he had his clothes, and pulled out the shorts. "I only have this kind. Is that okay?"

"Swim shorts?"

"Yeah, I use them for both," he said.

"That's good," Shane said. "I gather you swim then?"

"Yes," he said. "So, if you want to work in the pool and build some water exercises into my program, that works for me too."

"Will do," Shane replied.

When Keith was dressed and the crutches were under his armpits again, Shane shook his head. "Better leave the crutches here and bring the wheelchair."

Remembering his earlier words, Keith worried about it momentarily and then shrugged. "If you say so." He laid the crutches along the end of his bed, and, using the edge of the bed, made his way to where the wheelchair sat waiting for him. Once inside he wheeled out to the hallway. "Where are we going?"

"Down to one of the gyms," Shane said, walking beside him. "I want you doing some walking exercises first."

"I don't walk well," he warned.

"I know that," he said, "and you're still in a lot of pain. But we need to know which muscles are pulling harder and which ones are bailing on their job."

"They're all bailing," he said, "because the minute anybody even calls them out, somebody's hacking on them and sticking them elsewhere."

"Right," Shane said, flipping through the photos in his physical file. "Wow. You've really been put through the meat grinder, haven't you?"

"Frankenstein 2.0," he said cheerfully.

"Still, it's only bone and muscle," he said. "You have full function of all your organs, and, by the time we're done, you should walk and live a normal healthy life."

"If you say so," he said. He kept his voice deliberately neutral. He had given up hope a long time ago and couldn't let himself believe that progress could actually be made. After the roller coaster of so many surgeries, he had eventually gotten numb to it all. The last thing he wanted was any more surgery, and he told his doctor that.

At the time, the doctor had nodded and said, "Good thing we're done then, isn't it?"

He had tried to tell them earlier too, but the doctors hadn't listened because they had their own agenda as to what they wanted done. He was just the guy who had to suffer through it. He knew they were doing it for his own good and all, but having those words shoved down his throat enough times made him choke on them.

When he wheeled into the room that Shane pointed him to, Keith was surprised to see a beautiful hardwood floor, mats, all sorts of equipment and apparatuses, medicine balls, the whole works. "You guys didn't skimp on the equipment, did you?"

"You have no idea," Shane said. "A ton of equipment is in this place, and, believe it or not, we'll get to most of it eventually. But not for a while. A lot of work for you to do first."

"If you say so," he said. "Honestly, I'm not exactly sure how much I can even do."

"Which is why we'll work on it," he said, "because the one thing we don't want to do is have you short yourself on future abilities."

"Not sure there are any but whatever," he said.

"That attitude gets to be a little rough too," Shane said with a laugh. "You've got to feel something. Otherwise you feel nothing, and that's not good either."

"If you say so," he muttered under his breath, but he kept his voice fairly calm. No point in pissing off Shane too. An amazing amount of goodwill was here, and Keith didn't want to be the only jerk to them. It was just so hard when he was mentally so done with it all. He didn't care, had already given up, and that was a problem because he could see that Shane wanted him to care; Shane wanted Keith invested in his future. But it was hard to see a future when it didn't appear to be anything different than his present. And certainly he had nothing to celebrate here.

"Okay," Shane said. "First, I want you out of the wheelchair and on the mat, lying down on your back."

With a sideways look, Keith said, "I thought we were walking."

"We'll get there," Shane said, "but let's sort out your basic structure first."

"Whatever you say." Keith followed instructions. It was pretty interesting because Shane came at it from a way that was unexpected—nothing anybody had ever done before. It was certainly educational because, by the time Keith was listening and following through on the instructions, he could see what Shane was pointing out.

"When you are lying down, it's a whole different thing than the way you would be standing," Shane explained. "Straighten out your legs, and pull your legs together," Shane said. Then he took several photos, muttering to himself as he wrote down notes.

"Are you telling me that, even laying down, it's not even normal?" Keith joked.

"Nope, not really," he said. "That's why we're starting this on the floor. And then we'll get you standing upright. We'll have you walk, and we'll have you stand against a wall, while I take more measurements and more pictures."

At that, Keith relaxed because Shane really wouldn't put him to work today. But minutes later, Keith was eating his words because just doing what Shane was asking him to do was hard. But Shane didn't appear to be too bothered.

"I know I asked you to stand on one leg, and you're not used to it, but you can do it," he said. "So do it for me. Lean against that wall upright, heels to the back, and lift your left leg. Just balance."

But of course he couldn't keep balancing.

Finally Shane gave him a crutch and said, "Use this to help hold yourself up." And, with that, they went over it again and then again.

"What is it you're hoping to sort out?" Keith asked, gasping when he finally brought his leg back down again, feeling his back being pulled.

"Muscles that are avoiding working," he said. "You need your structural integrity solid. Otherwise, over time, you start to lean and to list to one side, and some muscles go weak, while others take on too much of the strain. As you age, these injuries become a bigger problem. We want to make sure that you start off healing correctly and get you solid with the best alignment you can have. Then we'll build up from there, so that—in twenty, thirty, forty, fifty years—you're not a basket case and back in a wheelchair."

"That doesn't sound like fun at all," he muttered. But, when Shane asked him to bend over and touch his toes, Keith just looked at him in shock.

"Go down as low as you can get and stretch as far as you can," Shane said.

But he could barely even get his hands to his knees.

Once again Shane was there, poking at the muscles in his back, taking photos and measurements. By the time they were done with the session, Keith was panting and wishing that he was already sitting down in his wheelchair.

Finally Shane let him sit down. "I don't know what any of that tells you," Keith said, "but we've done nothing except test yet again, and I'm exhausted."

"That's because I asked you to put some of the muscles under a spotlight," Shane said quietly, as he finished marking notes down on his tablet. "This is a big help," he said. "It gives me a really good idea where we need to start." At that, he motioned at the door and said, "We've been at it for an hour and a half, so I'll let you head back to your room. You've got some doctor appointments this afternoon, and I'll go set up your PT program. We'll start first thing in the morning at nine o'clock, so be ready."

"Where do I meet you?" Keith asked.

"Right here," he said. "We'll start on the floor again, but it will be a very different scenario tomorrow." And, with that dire warning, Shane was gone.

Back in his wheelchair, after crawling all the way across the floor and pulling himself into the chair, he was miffed that Shane had left him in that shape. But Keith had been on his feet for a lot of that time, so it's not like he was completely crippled.

He slowly moved back to his room and to his tablet to check on his next meeting. He wasn't even sure who it was, but it was some doctor something or other. Weren't they all doctors here?

As he wheeled into his room, he found a tall, angular midfifties woman, working on her tablet in a chair beside his bed. She looked up when he entered. "Keith?"

He nodded.

"Good," she said, reaching out a hand. "Don't get comfortable. We'll head back to my office." And, with that, she came around behind him, grabbed the wheelchair, and headed out into the hallway.

"Where is your office?" he asked, figuring out what doctor this was.

"This one here," she said, and she pushed him down a short hallway on the right. She wheeled him inside an open door on the left, parked him in front of her desk. Then she walked around to her side and, dropping the tablet, sat down in her chair. "So tell me," she said, "where are you at mentally with all this?"

Now he knew what kind of doctor she was. His heart sank. "I think I'm fine mentally," he said slowly, his mind immediately searching for the answers that would get her off his back.

She smiled. "You don't even know what I'm looking for, so no sense in digging around, trying to say the right thing to get rid of me."

He stared at her with a frown. "How did you know I was doing that?"

"Because you're in a chair across from me," she said with a quiet snicker. "Everybody tries to do exactly the same thing."

"That's not a very good way to make friends, you know?" he said.

"If I was on that side of the desk with you," she said, "I would be trying to make friends with you. But I'm on this side of the desk, and my job is to assess your mental health."

He frowned at that.

She nodded. "You have a very morose frame of mind. Your file says that you refused antidepressants and that you experience general downward-spiraling moods. We have a lot of clinical terms for this," she said, "but basically it means you're always on the edge of being depressed."

"Maybe so," he said. "But, if I'm on the edge of being depressed, then I'm also on the edge of being happy," he said. "If it's a knife's edge, it can cut both ways."

She laughed at that. "Good," she said. "I like to see your brain snappy like that. It shows that someone is still in there and that somebody hasn't given up."

He stared at her in surprise. "Does being depressed mean I've given up?"

"No, not necessarily," she said. "But it often goes hand in hand. Sometimes people can't see their way out of a situation, so they get depressed, and it's a downward spiral after that."

"Maybe," he said. "I've wondered how much of my moods could be part of the constant medical cocktail I've been served."

"Interesting take," she said, taking notes. "And one I certainly won't argue with because, with the number of surgeries you've had, undoubtedly a variety of chemicals still circulate through your blood. When did you finish your last antibiotics?"

"Before I got here," he said absentmindedly. "But I'm still taking a couple pills."

She read them off from the information in front of her.

"If you say so. I don't know what the names are, but, if they're almost done too, it won't matter unless they are antidepressants." He shrugged. "Like you said, I don't take them," he said, his tone hardening. "I think my body has been through enough. I don't need more chemical inducements to interfere with what should be a natural process."

"And what is that natural process?"

"Adjustment," he said instantly.

"Adjustment of what?"

"My life. My physical body. The fact that maybe, if I'm lucky, there will be no more surgeries. The fact that I'm here.

The fact that I'm spending time with my sister for the first time in ten years. The fact that—" He shook his head.

"Go on," she said gently.

He glared at her.

She smiled. "Whenever you're ready."

He stared down at his fingers. Even his pinky finger had needed surgery to straighten up the bones.

"Just adjustments," he said quietly. "From what was before, to what was, to what I've just completed, to whatever it is that's now."

"And then there is whatever comes after this," she said.

He raised his head and looked at her thoughtfully. "It's hard for me to see that far out. For the longest time all I saw was surgery upon surgery upon surgery. Now I'm here, and I understand that this is recovery." He stared out the window. "But I don't know what I'm recovering *to*."

"Does it matter?"

"It should matter," he said, his voice dropping even further. "Going through all these surgeries and physical adjustments, so much pain, where I'm heading to really should matter."

"So why doesn't it?"

He stared down at his hands again, wondering at her line of questioning.

"If it should matter and it doesn't, why not?" she persisted.

"I think because I can't see it," he said, slowly raising his gaze to study her.

She had a dark blue gaze that saw way too much. But then she saw everybody who was already here, and, as such, she had seen way too much of other people's ailments, and he was just one more. "I'm surrounded by other people struggling to deal with their health," he said. "It just seems like so much more of the same."

"Meaning?"

"Meaning," he said, "I don't see any progress. I don't see anybody dancing around the hallways. I don't see what *was* for somebody who's now doing much better." The words had just burst free of his chest.

She stared at him in surprise, then nodded ever-so-slightly. "That's a really interesting point," she said. "Of course I see the progress in many people, but then I saw them when they initially got here. I've also said goodbye to an awful lot of people who have been here and have improved to the point that they have gone on to completely normal lives. But, of course, you, as a patient, only see the other patients as they are today."

"Exactly," he said. "Though you talk about all these people who have improved so much, I don't see them. They aren't here for me to see that kind of change. I don't have any friends here. I don't have anybody who was in terrible shape before and now is looking so much better. So, for me, it's just all these nebulous possibilities that you guys keep talking about. And honestly? I don't know if I sincerely believe it, or if you're just plain lying."

"Do people lie to you much?"

"People lie all the time," he said flatly.

"Doctors?"

He nodded. "Absolutely doctors. Sure, they need to do one more surgery. They need to do this. They need to do that, and yes, of course, it all went well. But the funny thing is, I still can't do very much at the end of the day."

"Which is why there are no more surgeries, I presume?"

"Actually, the doctor said he'd done the best he could at

this point."

"Good," she said. "Now you can walk away from that stage of your life and move right into this one."

"Which is why this is the one that I see," he said. "I don't have a clue about what comes after this."

"And that brings us right around to the same conversation," she nodded. "And, if I were to introduce you to some guys who have shown remarkable progress here, would you believe them? Or would you think that we lied to you again?"

"But I wouldn't have been the one to see them when they arrived," he said flatly. "So any change is change that other people say has happened and not what I've seen for myself."

"You have a black-and-white viewpoint, where you need to see everything for yourself, don't you?"

He shrugged. "I guess," he said. "At this point in time anyway. People are always talking about how much better everything will get, but I haven't seen it at any stage of the game. So now it's really hard for me to believe anybody."

"Why did you come to Hathaway House?"

He stared at her for a long moment until she nudged him again.

"I presume that you wanted to come. The fact that you're here should mean that you applied and went through the effort to come here because it was your choice."

"I came because of my sister," he said.

"Ouch," she said. "There's a huge waiting list for all the beds here, so please don't tell the other patients that."

He looked at her for a long moment and said, "Maybe somebody else should have my bed," he said, "because I sure don't know if I'm the right guy to be here."

"Why do you think that?"

"Because I've been through a lot in the name of progress and haven't seen any happening. So it's hard for me to imagine it's even possible. So I probably should just go back to the same VA place I was at before and let somebody else make good use of being here. I don't think I'm the right person at all." And, with that, he spun his wheelchair and headed out of the room.

Chapter 6

JUST ENOUGH OF an insider grapevine existed in a place like this that Ilse had heard about the bit of a disruption in Keith's world once he'd had the psych visit. But then she could understand why he wouldn't want anybody questioning what he said or saw or thought or felt. She just happened to be walking down the hallway to Dani's office, when she heard the sound of a wheelchair moving rapidly behind her. As she pivoted, she saw Keith turn into his room and slam the door behind him. Hard. She winced at that.

As she got to Dani's office, she was happy to find her in and not in a meeting.

Dani motioned to the chair across the desk, as she was on the phone. She quickly finished the call. "Problems?"

"Nope," Ilse said. "Just bringing up the budget and supply invoices for the last month." She handed them to Dani, who took a quick look.

"You always seem to be on target."

"That's the job," she said with a laugh. "You wouldn't like it if I came in saying I needed an extra fifteen hundred dollars this month."

"No, but it wouldn't surprise me," Dani said. "It seems like everybody needs an extra fifteen hundred dollars right now."

"Right," she said with a nod. "That was a pretty hard

door slam a few moments ago too," she said. "It was Keith, but I have no idea what's wrong."

Dani clicked her mouse, frowned at her monitor, and said, "Well, I have a pretty good idea," she said, "but I may go talk to him later, or maybe I'll just let him work his way through it."

"I guess a lot of that happens here, doesn't it? Just working their way through it, I mean."

"There is," Dani said, her tone serious. "These guys have issues that we can't even imagine. And yet they still manage to keep fighting the good fight. Even when I feel like I might have given up a long time ago."

"I was thinking that earlier today," Ilse said with a small smile. "I'm not sure I'd have the strength and the endurance to do what these guys are doing every day."

"I know," she said. "I watched my father for a long time. He'd get depressed and morose, angry—so angry at what life had done to him," she said. "It made growing up pretty rough over those last few years as he tried to heal. Once we started this center, and he had a purpose, something to work toward, it made a huge difference for him. But it really was seeing something beyond the immediate future that made a difference in his world."

"I can see that," Ilse said. "A lot of the current philosophy says forget about tomorrow, forget about yesterday, and just focus on today. But then, if today looks pretty bad, and you can't see that there'll be a tomorrow that's any better, it just makes for a really rough today."

"It usually takes a few weeks here," Dani said. "In some cases, as long as six weeks for the guys to realize that progress is really happening and that there really is hope for something beyond this. They come from these centers and hospitals, circumstances that are often less than ideal, or, at the very least, they've been allowed to wallow in the collective misery, so their mental attitude is way less than ideal. And it's not just a physical shift but a mental and an emotional shift here. They have to let go of all that stuff, and it's hard, really hard. A lot of them cling to it out of fear. Others cling to it like it's protecting them because it's what they know and is like a safeguard for when it just doesn't get any easier."

Ilse stood and said, "It's hard when somebody really hits you in the heart, and you see his struggles, and his daily strength amazes you."

"Keith again?"

Ilse nodded, shoving her hands in her pockets. "I've never had a patient here affect me like this."

"It may not ever happen again," Dani said. "You see it on a professional relationship level, as if something about him as a patient is really amazing to you," she said. "But it looks to me like you are seeing the man inside. That's why nobody else has affected you before, and nobody is likely to affect you in the future because something special is happening between the two of you. It's the same relationship elements as any male and female the world over experience."

Ilse looked at her in surprise. "It's hardly a place for personal relationships though," she said slowly.

But Dani was having none of that. "This place has been *very much* the place of personal relationships," she said with a boisterous laugh. "I mean, Aaron and I started it," she said, "but easily another maybe half a dozen to a dozen relationships have evolved ever since. I never expected to be a matchmaking service here, but we've certainly seen many happy couples."

"I wonder if Robin has introduced Iain to Keith at all," Ilse said suddenly. "Maybe if Keith saw how Iain is now, it would give Keith some hope that maybe he could improve too."

"I suspect he's one of those guys who wouldn't believe the change because he didn't see Iain before."

Ilse winced. "You could be right," she said. She walked to the doorway. "You got all your paperwork, and I'm good now, right?"

Dani quickly flipped through the pages. "You're good."

"Perfect," she said. "I'm off to make sure dinner is on time."

"Good luck with that," Dani said. "Honestly, I don't know how you do it. I have enough trouble cooking for myself, without trying to cook for hundreds, like you are."

"It's what we do," Ilse said with a laugh, waved goodbye, and headed down the hallway.

As she walked past Keith's room, she froze for a moment, and wondered. Unable to help herself, she reached out and knocked on his door. But instead of a cheery "Hello" or a "Come in," it was a stern "Go away."

At that, she frowned and said, "That's not a very nice thing to say, you know?" She hesitated, remaining outside the door.

After a dead silence for a moment, he spoke, a grudging, "Come in."

Knowing she was confronting the bear in his cave, she pushed open the door but stayed outside the doorway. "Obviously you've had a rough afternoon," she said gently.

He just glared at her.

"I'm not pitying you," she said, raising both hands. "That would be the last thing I'd do. I just wondered if maybe a cup of coffee and a piece of pie or something would make you feel the tiniest bit better."

He stared at her in astonishment, and a glimmer of humor appeared in his eyes, until he was suddenly chuckling. "Is that your solution to everything?" he teased.

"Hey, it works in my world," she said, relieved to see his dark mood lifting.

"You're right," he said. "Coffee and pie would be absolutely perfect." He looked around at the bed that he'd finally managed to get himself back into. "The trouble is, I don't think I can go out there again. Not right now."

"Don't have to," she said. "I've still got a few minutes. I'll go grab you a piece." She started to leave, then stopped and turned back. "Do you want ice cream on the pie?"

"Is the pope Catholic?" he asked with a twinkle in his eye.

Responding with a giant eye roll, she said, "I presume that means yes." She quickly walked down the hallway, but now she was the one wearing a big grin. Maybe she couldn't do a whole lot for him, but just the fact that she'd gotten a smile out of him was a huge turning point.

Back in her kitchen, she cut a piece of apple pie, put a scoop of vanilla ice cream on it, then added a couple blackberries on the top. Pouring a cup of coffee, she disappeared again, ignoring the grins of everyone around her. She didn't care what they thought or that they would gossip about it after she left because, if this simple act would make one person in this place feel better, then she was all for it. The whole thing had given her a new appreciation of the food that she put out for these people. She saw with fresh eyes just how much it could mean to them to know something like an apple pie awaited them at the end of a particularly rough day.

As she approached his room, she realized the door was still open. She had left it open, knowing she was coming right back. As she stepped through, she said, "I'm sorry about leaving your door open."

"It's fine," he said. "This way I don't have to growl at you again to open it."

She burst out laughing as she walked over and placed the treats on the table, then moved the table across the bed. "That's a good point," she said. "I've got older brothers, so you don't scare me."

He looked at her with interest. "Are they as small as you?"

She chuckled. "No, they sure aren't. They're big. Both of them are six foot tall, and they used to call me Pint Pot all of my growing up years. It was totally embarrassing." Yet she smiled at the memory. "But, as older brothers do, they also protected me, looked after me, and completely spoiled me."

"Sounds like you have a good relationship with them." He looked at the pie, plucked a blackberry off the top, and took a bite. "What is it about something like this treat midafternoon on a bad day that just brightens everything up?"

"Because food is the nectar of the gods," she announced. "I learned how to soothe the most savage of beasts of my brothers with food, so I highly doubt anybody here in this place is any worse."

He chuckled and used his fork to break off a piece of the apple pie with some ice cream and put it in his mouth. He put the fork down and melted against the sheets. "I was in such a bad mood before," he said, "and, seriously, your little bit of kindness has gone a long way to making my day better." He lifted the coffee cup. "Cheers."

She smiled, walked back out, and, as she turned by the door, said, "Well, let's hope the rest of your day is better." Inside, she was thrilled, and her own heart was considerably warmer too because she felt happiness when doing something nice for somebody else—but to also know it was appreciated meant so much.

There really was a special connection between the two of them, even though she'd been determined to keep it more formal, but it was well past that now. She really liked him. The fact that he wasn't capable of doing anything more than lying in the bed and just talking to her also kept it in perspective. She didn't want to do anything to distract or to disturb him, but she really wanted to do everything she could to help him heal, and maybe then there'd be something between them at the end of the day, and they could explore it a little more too.

THE APPLE PIE had been absolutely divine. Keith didn't know if she made it or if one of her sous chefs had, but, wow, the filling had been thick and rich. The pastry was fluffy and flaky. And, by the time his plate was empty, he was wishing he'd asked her for more. It was hardly fair to ask for seconds, but, at the same time, he just couldn't resist having this treat. He didn't think he had much of a sweet tooth, but she was proving him wrong. And, of course, the coffee was always good.

He sank back against the bed, wondering at his mercurial moods these days. Before it had never been a problem because he'd always just been depressed. He hated to even say it because saying that he'd been depressed would just make things worse. No way he was depressed, but it just made him feel better to avoid that label, and that was difficult too. Critical moods meant that his moods were shifting.

Before he had been filled with a total apathy, a sense of weightiness maybe, and an acceptance that nothing would change. But now, instead of always feeling that same dark moodiness, he found these pockets of bright laughter that he didn't even know what to do with.

He stared down at his hands, wondering, when a knock came at his open door. He looked up to see his sister. She had a big grin on her face and something in her arms that he couldn't even believe. "What the heck is that?" he exclaimed.

She laughed and walked to his bedside. "I don't want to put him on top of you if he's too heavy."

He shifted in the bed as she laid down the largest rabbit he'd ever seen in his life. Immediately the rabbit hopped forward, its big nose, monstrous eyes, and huge ears heading toward Keith's face, looking to sniff him closer. He reached out a gentle hand, letting the rabbit sniff it; then he gently tugged on one of its long silky ears.

"This is Hoppers," Robin said in a bright tone.

He looked up at her, down at the rabbit, and asked, "Why?"

"Why what?" she said, laughing.

"Why would somebody give this rabbit nuclear steroids so he looks like this?" he said in disbelief. "It's as big as I am."

"Not quite," she said.

At that moment, Hoppers stretched right out, as if really enjoying Keith's bed. Dropping his head down beside

Keith's waist, Hoppers snuggled in.

"Good Lord," he said in astonishment, but he couldn't stop touching him. "He's beautiful. And is he always this calm?"

"Always," she said, with a roll of her eyes. "He's a semi-permanent resident."

"How does somebody become a semipermanent resident?" he asked, frowning at her.

"He didn't used to be here, but he's so big that he requires a certain amount of care, and we haven't found the right adoptive home, so we've built a run for him. Or rather, Iain did."

"Ah, the mythical Iain," Keith said. "I have yet to meet this guy. You know that, right?"

"I'd love for you to meet him," she said warmly. "He was in the same position as you were not that many months ago. I forget how far he has come."

"He probably wasn't quite so bad though," he said.

"He was bad, Keith," she said.

Something in her tone made him look up and study her face. "How bad?"

"Different than you but ugly bad," she said. "I did wonder, for a long time, if I could handle a relationship like that," she said. "I didn't feel very good about having those questions go through my mind, but the good news is that Iain is in wonderful shape now. He's recovered beautifully, and—even if, down the road, he has a setback and ends up in a wheelchair again—I already know that I can handle it. Those thoughts came in fleeting moments of doubting myself, wondering if I was capable, if I was a big enough person to do this. I can tell you that I'm just so happy to have found him."

And, indeed, she was positively glowing. He'd never seen his sister like that. "He appears to have had a pretty strong effect on you," he said in surprise. "I've never seen you look so happy."

She nodded. "And that's exactly it," she said. "I am happy. More than that, I'm thrilled with the way my life has turned out."

"Are you still happy to be working with animals?"

She chuckled. "I'm taking my buddy Hoppers to visit the patients and my brother," she said. "How hard can my life be?"

"Yes, but any given morning you might have to put a dog to sleep," he said. "And I know the little girl I watched grow up would find that to be very difficult."

"It was a cat this morning," she said with a sad smile. "She got hit by a car. We couldn't save her."

"I'm sorry," he said gently.

She nodded. "Unfortunately we have to put animals down on a regular basis. We do the best we can, but we aren't infallible." She looked at him with searching eyes. "Just like you. The doctors did the best they could, but they aren't infallible either."

He winced at that. "Thanks for the reminder."

"You're welcome," she said. "You know the animals also remind me of how much we can do. We took the leg off a pup this morning that was so badly damaged he was dragging it behind him. Our plan is to put a peg into it down the road. At the moment it's healing, and, when it's better, we'll get him set up. He's got a big screw-pin system, so we'll pop on a leg and adjust it for the right height, and that guy will barely even notice."

"Is it that simple?"

"No," she said, "but it's not that much harder."

Her words resonated long after she left. He curled up with the blanket, his hand still resting where the animal had laid on his bed. One of the orderlies had come in and asked if he wanted his sheets changed because of the bunny hair. He had immediately shook his head and told him that tomorrow would be soon enough.

Smiling, the man had given Keith an understanding nod and left.

But Keith had to wonder if he could finally adjust, as all the animals did. Even his sister did because she hadn't been the person to deal with hurt and injured animals, but even she had seen enough good-ending stories to make her have a positive outlook on the work that she did. And, if she could do that, maybe there was hope for him too.

The empty plate in front of him caught his eye. He wished he could go down and grab another piece of pie, but he could hear his long-deceased mother's voice in the back of his head, telling him not to bother because it would ruin his dinner.

And, for the first time in a long time, he smiled without any other reason than because he wanted to.

Chapter 7

THAT WAS THE pattern for the next couple weeks. Ilse was surprised to see Keith awake every morning to the point that one day she teased him and said, "Awake again? Are you sure you aren't waiting for me to come in every day?"

His answer seemed to surprise him just as much because he responded immediately with, "Absolutely, I am."

They both stared at each other for a long moment, understanding and pleasure evident on both their faces. She couldn't help smiling. "How is the progress here?"

"Coming along," he said, but his tone was reserved, and he didn't give much information.

"Good," she said. "I'll be by with some coffee in a bit." She headed to her kitchen. Something was just so special about that connection on a regular basis with Keith. Something she didn't even really know what to do with but just provide it with water and nurture it so it could grow.

When she walked into the kitchen that morning, she was surprised to see Ricky here. Scared to ask, but knowing she had to, she looked at him. "And?"

He beamed. "It's not leukemia." At that moment, he threw himself into her arms and gave her a big hug. He was laughing and crying at the same time. "I couldn't wait to tell you," he said. "I'll bake up a storm today," he cried out, joyfully turning around in circles, his arms wide. "I love it when I get to bake."

"Maybe," she said cautiously, "but make sure you spread out the goodies for a few days. And don't slip on the paperwork."

He laughed. "And that's fine too," he said. "Thank you so much for giving me these days. It meant so much that I could be there for my family, and I'm just so grateful that my daughter will be okay."

"Good," she said.

When the other kitchen crew members arrived, they all heard the good news too. Then she realized that, once again, she'd forgotten Keith's coffee. She quickly made more and took a cup to Keith. His door was shut when she got there. She knocked lightly, but she got no response and heard no sounds inside. Not wanting to disturb him, she walked past his room. It was still early, but there could be any number of reasons why the door was closed. She headed back to the kitchen, sipping the coffee as if it were her own.

When she walked back in with the cup, her staff looked at her and frowned.

"His door was closed," she said by way of explanation.

"Was that a first?"

"Yes," she said, "but there's a first for everything, I suppose." And she put it out of her mind and got to work.

Two hours later she thought of it again. She looked down at her watch and noted it was nearly eight o'clock. Without even giving herself a chance to question what she was doing, she poured another cup of coffee and headed to his room again. Once more she found the door closed. She frowned, knocked again, and still got no answer.

Shane walked toward her as she turned away from the

door.

"Is he okay?" she asked.

He looked at her in surprise. "Is there a reason he wouldn't be?"

"I don't think so." She shrugged and said, "I've just gotten in the habit of bringing him coffee, but his door has been closed all day."

"Wow," he said. "You know I could get in the habit of you bringing me coffee too," he said with a big grin.

She rolled her eyes. "No," she said. "You are perfectly capable of going down there and getting coffee yourself."

At that, he reached out and grabbed her hand gently. "You do know that he is too, right?"

She nodded and said, "I know. Originally I was just being welcoming and making his first few days here a bit easier, and then it just became a habit."

"Sounds like a nice habit for him, as long as you're not putting yourself out."

"Of course not," she said. "He's not answering my knock on his door today, so I'll just leave him be. I'll talk to you later." She walked away. She didn't really want everybody making too big of a deal out of this, but she was sad at not seeing Keith.

As she got to the end of the hallway she heard knocking and watched as Shane waited at Keith's door. When he got no answer, he turned the knob and stepped in. She wasn't even sure what had happened, but the next thing she knew was an alarm sounded through the building. She stood in the corner of the hallway and watched in amazement as several people raced toward Keith's room, and she realized there must be a problem.

With her heart in her throat, she stood there with a cup

of coffee, sipping it, waiting for news, worried that something major must have happened. When others came back out again, they were laughing and talking, so it couldn't have been all that bad. But she stayed rooted in place until Shane came out.

He took one look at her and walked toward her rapidly. Reaching her, he touched her shoulder. "He's fine," he said. "He's just fine."

She took several slow, deep breaths. "What happened?"

"It looks like he tried to get out of bed and fell."

She frowned. "And the door closed?"

"I think he was trying to get into the wheelchair, and it skittered away and likely caught the door and closed it because the wheelchair was up against the door."

She nodded slowly. "And he's okay?"

"He hit his head when he went down. When I went in, he was just coming out of it. So he's completely off the schedule today with orders not to leave the bed, so all meals need to be delivered."

"Of course," she said, quietly staring at the room behind him. "Now I feel really bad. What if he was already on the floor at five o'clock this morning?"

"No," Shane said, "that wouldn't have happened. He'd probably just fallen back to sleep."

"Maybe." Then it wasn't just her who went to his room. Orderlies and nurses did any number of routine checks all throughout the day and night. "Do you think it's okay if I go in and see him?"

"I think so," he said thoughtfully. "Come on. I'll go with you."

The two of them walked to Keith's room. The door was open now, and Keith was lying in bed, looking a little worse for wear. He looked up, saw her, and frowned.

"I knocked on the door," she said, "and you didn't answer. I was terrified something was wrong."

"Are you the reason that Shane found me?"

She shook her head. "I did tell him, but he was already at the door, looking for you."

"Yeah," he said. "Apparently I was trying to walk before I can crawl." He shook his head and turned to face the window.

"And I forgot to bring you coffee, so I was bringing this one," she said, "and then I just drank it because it was getting cold." At that point, she stared lamely down at the empty cup.

Hearing a whisper of sound, she turned to see Shane heading out, talking on his phone as he walked. She looked over at Keith. "Can I bring you another cup?"

He looked at her in surprise. "I was coming down to get a cup. I failed at that too."

She looked at him for a long moment, nodded, and said, "You know what? The thing is, when we fail, we still have to get up and try again."

"Not for a day or two," he said. "Apparently I'm confined to bed right now anyway."

"I'll get you a cup of coffee," she said. "It sounds like you could use it." And before she left, she said, "Remember that you tried. Even if you did fail, at least you tried." And, with that, she turned and left.

IT SHOULD MATTER that he tried, but somehow the failure seemed to be the bigger part of this. Keith wasn't even sure how it happened. He had straightened, had slipped off the bed, and had suddenly gotten dizzy, grabbed for the bed rail in order to stop himself from falling, but the chair, the bed, and the table had shifted, and he'd gone down. Even his attempt to save himself had been a disaster, as he caught his own foot going down, and he'd hit his head. The fact that he'd knocked himself out was something he didn't want to think about. He'd never been the clumsy type. He'd never been the kind to have accidents or to fall and to wipe out like that. To be found by somebody else, well that was just the worst.

Had she found him? He racked his brain, trying to remember what she'd said. Shane had been there at the same time, so maybe, maybe not. He hoped not. Because that was just another dent to his pride. The fact that he was even worried about his pride with a woman was something he didn't even want to consider, but it was hard to not see that something was developing between them.

He knew he should cut it off and stop it right now because he couldn't be the person she wanted him to be. No way he could be the man whom she needed, the man whom she deserved. His days of filling that role were long gone, and it broke his heart because, for the first time in a long time, he'd met somebody he cared enough to want to be there for. It was wrong, and it was maddening that he would be in this position, finding somebody so special. But, because she was special, he also knew that he had to let her go. It would break his heart to do it, but he wouldn't let her waste her time with a useless chump like him.

He also knew that everybody else around him would have a heyday with his mental state. And that just showed him once again what a rough time he'd had of it. But this wasn't about self-pity. This was about coming to terms with reality. Whether she liked it or not, this might be fine for the moment, but, down the road, it wouldn't be anywhere near good enough.

Why would it be? Lots of others—better, healthier, and stronger men than him were out there. And he could do only so much in replacing the person who he used to be. That physically fit, strong male who he had been wasn't part of his repertoire anymore, and he would have to let that go.

He'd already let it go to some extent. He was well past the point of hoping to be what he used to be, that longing for who he was, but he didn't know how he could get her to understand that. And it also meant denying himself something that he desperately wanted, which was time with her. He didn't know what it was, but something about her just made him feel good to be around her. Something about her presence made him feel special, even to spend a few minutes talking with her. He looked forward to seeing her in the morning to the point that he now woke up just so that he could see her and could hopefully spend time with her. It wasn't even five minutes, but it was just that connection in the morning, and then her bringing coffee back later on.

When one of the nurses shut the door as she left this morning, he'd stared at that closed door, wondering if his coffee would come, or if that was some sign too. And it had been a sign all right. A sign that he was an idiot. A sign that he would never be what he had always hoped he could be. How ridiculous was that?

He shook his head, determined to put it away inside him. When she walked back in again, bringing him coffee, he nodded politely and said, "Thank you."

"You're welcome." She left the cup for him, stopped,

and then said, "And, no, it makes no bit of difference." Then she turned and walked out.

He watched her stiff back. It was almost as if she'd seen his thoughts. How did that work? It's not supposed to work at all. He didn't understand, but obviously she'd seen something, somehow, and he didn't like it. Didn't like it one bit.

Chapter 8

ILSE DIDN'T KNOW why she'd walked away, but something had been in Keith's gaze. He wouldn't look at her, as if he were ashamed. She didn't have a whole lot of patience with that. He needed to fully embrace the self-pity or drop it permanently. Accept it or leave it. But she couldn't understand the hanging on to it. Maybe he had been embarrassed and humiliated over the whole falling incident, but it was a minor thing to her. And, of course, because it was minor to her, it didn't matter, but that didn't make it minor to him.

Acknowledging that, she headed back to work. But it stewed away inside her brain and heart until the next morning, when she walked past his room as usual, but no light was on under his closed door. She quickly slipped down the hallway, wondering if he'd had a bad night, and maybe he didn't sleep, or if he was finally sleeping through the night. Either way the next morning and the one after that were the same thing, and, by then, she knew that he was avoiding her.

She groaned at that. Because she really, really cared about him. Yet she also could see that he wouldn't be an easy person to be around.

As she was leaving for a couple hours on her own time, she saw Robin outside with the horses. She walked over and said, "Hi, how are you doing?"

"Good," she said. "Iain is coming by this weekend for a visit. That'll be nice."

"Good," she said. "Maybe you can get your brother to see him. He's pretty cranky and miserable these days."

Robin shot a sideways look. "You two seem pretty close."

"Well, we were," Ilse said sadly. "Until he had the fall a few days ago. And now it's like he's shutting me out." At that, she laughed. "Look at me. I'm making a big deal out of nothing. It's just that every morning I've been stopping by his room to see if he's awake, as he's been waking early, and then I come back with coffee and spend a few minutes with him," she said. "And I really liked that time with him, and I think he did too. But the last three mornings, his light hasn't been on, and either he's been sleeping or pretending to be asleep."

"Interesting," Robin murmured. "He's not an easy person to get along with."

"Yeah," Ilse said. "I noticed."

She laughed. "He wasn't always like this," she said, "but our mother died when we were young, and then our father ended up with a new wife. As soon as Keith turned sixteen, our father showed him the door and told him that he was a man now, and he could get out on his own."

Ilse looked at her in shock.

Robin nodded. "I was pretty upset and screamed about it all, but I got backhanded for my trouble. His new wife was pregnant, and he wanted to have his new family, not his old family. As it was, Keith had a friend. The guy had a room over his garage with a little kitchenette. Keith moved in there, and I don't think he and our father ever spoke again. I went back and forth constantly between my home and Keith's apartment. And then he joined the military, and I basically moved into the same little room he had just vacated.

"I had just turned sixteen then, and, although my father told me that I had a room at his house until I was eighteen, I was thumbing my nose at him, telling him that I didn't want it. If Keith couldn't stay, I wasn't staying either." She laughed. "Looking back now, I guess I was pretty stubborn and stuck-up, but I was hurting because my brother had been taken from me in a way that I hadn't been ready for yet."

"That adds some understanding as to why your brother is so dark."

"He was always pretty moody after our mother's death. He was very close to her," she said. "Our father didn't have an easy way of handling it. He pretty well ignored us, went out, got drunk all the time, and partied. And the next thing we know, he's bringing home a new wife."

"Ooh, ouch," Ilse said. She just couldn't imagine how much trauma that would have caused for a young man. "At least in the military he would have ended up with a family of his own," she said. "That should have helped."

"I think it did help a lot," she said. "When I saw him afterward, he seemed more settled. Happier somehow. As if he'd found something that he'd been missing. Of course that just made me feel like he didn't want me either. Because, if he'd found something, and it wasn't me, then it was something else." Robin chuckled. "But I was more adjusted than he was, and that made life none too easy either."

"Of course not," she said. "Still, I hurt for your whole family. What about your father now? Do you have anything to do with him?"

"Oddly enough, he reached out not too long ago because he's going through a divorce," she said in a wry tone. "And his wife wants child support for the two children he gave her."

"Of course," she said. "And probably wants sole custody. So he doesn't want the divorce or the limited visitation when he has to pay child support, right?"

"I think he's realizing that he not only lost his first family but he's now in danger of losing his second family."

"Yep," Ilse said, "I've seen that happen time and time again."

"I know, and it's sad, but it is what it is," she said. "I don't think he's reached out to Keith at all. And I'm not sure Keith would have anything to do with him if he did."

"Depends on if he can forgive and move on," she said. "Not everything in life is quite so dark."

"I don't know. I think, in Keith's case, it certainly is," she said. "After the accident that put him in the hospital, he also lost one friend at the time and another friend about three months ago. After months and months of rehab and everybody thought his buddy was good, then a blood clot or something like that came loose and took him. I know since then that Keith, who doesn't talk about it at all, has been pretty quiet. As if all that effort that his friend made was completely useless, so what's the point?"

"Yeah, that's how he was when he fell too," she said.

"I didn't hear about the fall," Robin said with a frown.

"No, not many people did. He tried to get into the wheelchair or grab his crutches or something. I'm not sure. He was going to get a coffee for himself, but somehow he ended up falling and hitting his head on the floor, knocking himself out. We don't think he was out for very long though," Ilse said. "He was put on bed rest for a couple days, but he should be back up and moving around again now."

Robin nodded. "And of course he probably asked that nobody tell me about it," she said in a wry tone. "That would be so him."

"Well, I hate to say that it's possible, but it sounds quite probable," Ilse said.

"Yeah, he doesn't like anybody fussing over him," Robin said. "So that's a warning. If you ever show any pity or try to coddle him, he'll back off right away."

"I don't think I did that," she said, "but he's definitely backed off, and I have to admit that I'm kind of angry about it."

"Good," Robin said robustly. "Get angry, and let him know that you're angry. He cuts people out of his life because either they hurt him or he's afraid they'll be hurt by him."

And those words resonated long after Ilse left Robin with the horses. Even for another few days.

When she went in Monday morning, she saw a light on in his room. She stopped, not sure she should say hi or not. But she decided to try it. She knocked on the door lightly.

He looked up and smiled and said, "I haven't seen you in a week," he said.

"I wondered if you were pretending to be asleep when I came by," she said, opting for the truth.

His lids fell closed slightly, confirming her suspicions.

"I'm not sure what I did," she said lightly, as she moved into the room. "Or why you've decided to forgive me and say hi now."

"I missed you," he said simply.

At that, her heart melted yet again. "You know how to break apart somebody's defenses, don't you?"

He chuckled. "I didn't realize you had any," he said. "You've always been the sweetest, nicest person, and, well, it's hard for me to realize just how nice you are versus how not so nice I am."

She stared at him for a moment, her arms crossing over her chest, and she tapped her foot. "That better not be more self-pity," she said.

"And why is that?" he asked, his gaze flying to her face.

"Because that's one of the hardest things for anybody else to deal with. You need to toss that one off and walk away from it."

"You make it sound so easy," he said.

"No, it's not," she said, "but it's not impossible. I never think in terms of what somebody can do for me or what somebody has got going that somebody else doesn't. I don't make comparisons," she said. "Obviously something is between us, and we like each other's company. We love spending time together, and I think it's important to see where that will go," she said. "But I would just as soon do it coming from a position of truth and trust."

His gaze widened slightly, and he nodded. "I like the sound of that," he said. Then he smiled. "But just because I take a step forward doesn't mean I'm not taking a step back."

"And," she said, "just because you fall or fail once doesn't mean you don't try again."

"Deal," he said, and then he chuckled. "What's the chance of getting a coffee this morning?"

"So, is it me you wanted to see," she teased, "or just my coffee?"

His booming laughter rang out through the room, and

she was afraid they would wake up the other patients. She walked to the door and said, "Be back in ten. Or not," she said with a roll of her eyes. "You never know what I'll find when I hit the kitchen."

He chuckled and nodded.

She headed to the kitchen with a smile on her face. It was nice to have him back.

KEITH LISTENED TO her footsteps as she walked down the hallway, his heart much lighter, and his soul wearing a smile for the first time ever. He thought about all the other areas in his life that were so messed up. Yet this one particular area may have just straightened itself out. He wasn't sure how he'd gone from trying to tell her that she needed to find somebody else to warming to everything she had to say, desperately wanting to be the person who could follow through on it.

Had he really been cutting himself short? She hadn't implied that, but she certainly had no patience with self-pity. Was he that kind of a person? Maybe he hadn't been giving his all. And that hurt too. But he was willing to give it a try and to see what he could do. And that just brought up the email he got from his father. He had absolutely no freaking idea how the old man even knew what his email address was. But he half suspected that Robin was behind it. His father was getting a divorce and somehow realized, as he faced the loss of his second family, that maybe he'd already lost the first one, and it might be too late. But, if it wasn't too late, could his son possibly respond and let him know that he was alive?

Keith hadn't answered, and now it just sat in the back of his mind, festering. He wasn't ready to talk to his father. He wasn't ready to open up any more wounds. And his father, of course, wouldn't have a clue. He probably had no idea that Keith had even been injured. Then again, with Robin around, his dad definitely might know. But their dad probably didn't know the details because Robin was as loyal as she was caring.

She might have said that Keith had been hurt in the military and was recovering. But who knew? He should give his dad a chance to find out, but Keith had to look after himself, and enough was shaking loose in his world these days that Keith wasn't sure he was ready to open up that Pandora's box too.

It didn't sound very nice on his part, to see his father as a problem, but Keith knew that his emotional state, although getting stronger by the day, was also still very fragile. And Keith hated that. But what he didn't want was to have any more setbacks that would slide him backward emotionally either.

Midmorning, when Shane came by, he carried some big files. Keith looked at them and asked, "What's all that?"

"Progress," Shane said. "Progress that you need to see but probably wouldn't, unless you could see the black-and-white of it."

Keith stared at him and said, "You going to talk or will you show me what's in there?"

Shane burst out laughing. "Well, I'll show you." He laid it out on the bed carefully across Keith's knees and said, "These are the photos that I took that first day you and I had an appointment. That set of testing, where you were grumbling about how tired you were from doing nothing."

Keith looked down at the pictures and winced. "Wow," he said, "those are really ugly."

"Well, nobody said I was a great photographer either," Shane said, deliberately misunderstanding him. Then he continued, "This one is at three weeks."

He held out a photo that was marginally better. The leg looked a little bit fuller, less angry.

"Now this is the one I took yesterday." He picked up another photo, and he laid it down farther from Keith. "In this picture, what do you see that's different?"

Keith stared at the pictures, as he studied the simple image of him sitting on a bench. There were two bench photos, both taken when Keith had been unaware. In the first one he listed to the side, his body inflamed and in obvious pain, but, in the last one, he sat up straighter, more muscle having developed on his left side, whereas it had been crunched in on that first photo. The color of his leg was more even-toned now, and the muscle obviously less inflamed, to the point of being almost happy.

"Wow," he said, "that's a really nice picture. I wasn't expecting to see that kind of change."

"It's one of the reasons I document the progress with photos," Shane said, "because, if *you* don't see it, *you* don't believe it. This is a godsend for you because seriously you're already there, showing improvement," he said. "This should show you that the work we're doing has value."

"I always knew it had value," Keith said. "I just didn't realize how much and how soon."

"Of course not," Shane replied. "But this? This is gold. So, are you going to give me any more guff about progress?"

Keith looked up in shock, smiled, and shook his head. "Absolutely not. Thank you. I really needed this." He looked at the photos, then at Shane, and asked, "Can I keep them?"

"They're yours," he said, "for whatever you need to do with them."

"Perfect," he said. "Thank you."

Chapter 9

THE NEXT MORNING, when Ilse walked into Hathaway House, she headed straight for Keith's room. As she walked toward it, she could see his light shining, and she grinned. Her heart lightened as she stuck her head in the doorway and said, "So, is this like a standing date now?"

He chuckled. "Well, I tried to ignore you, and it didn't work."

He was sitting up this morning, looking at a bunch of photos. She hesitated to step forward because she hadn't been invited, but he lifted his head, looked at her, and crimped his finger.

"Come here and see what Shane brought."

She could see that he had laid out progress pictures. She picked up the first one, wincing. "Dear God," she said, "what your poor body has been through."

He nodded and said, "Now hold that photo next to this one from yesterday."

She looked at the two in surprise. "Wow," she said. "All that inflammation and the angry-looking welts and redness are gone. The muscles are fuller, healthier looking, thicker."

"And look at these two," he said, holding up the ones where he's sitting on the bench.

"Oh, my God," she said. "The first one looks like you're in terrible pain," she whispered.

"And the second one?"

She looked at it and smiled. "You're sitting up straighter, much more of a military posture, and, while I'm not saying you're happy in that picture," she said cautiously because really he didn't look happy, "but you look better."

"Exactly. I don't look happy because I still have a ton of work to be done, but, in the first one, I was in a ton of pain and a lot of that was due to my poor posture because I was collapsing in on myself. The muscles weren't capable of holding me up, but now I'm feeling like I can do so much more," he said enthusiastically.

She chuckled, laid the photos back down, and said, "So, at five o'clock in the morning, this is what you're doing?"

"Absolutely," he said, "and chances are I should be doing it every morning for the rest of my life."

"Not a bad idea. Success begets more success, whether small or large," she said, as she walked back to the doorway. "Back in ten with coffee." And she quickly strode down the hallway, feeling so happy for him. It was obvious that he was full of pride and bursting with accomplishment. She knew he still had a long way to go, but she was still stuck on how injured and vulnerable he had looked in the first set of pictures. She'd met him already at that time, but he had been in bed, covered up, and so she hadn't seen the kind of damage that had been done to his body, both to harm and to heal. The images wouldn't leave her alone, even as she made coffee and greeted her staff as they came in one by one, got the kitchen started, and then as she headed back to deliver a coffee to Keith.

"We've got to stop meeting like this," he said, as she walked into his room.

"Why?" she said lightly. "It appears to be working for

us."

A smile slipped out of the corner of his mouth. "Good point," he said. "Okay, I was just feeling guilty that you keep doing this."

"Hey, I like seeing you first thing in the morning, before the world is awakened, before your full schedule starts, and before my kitchen goes crazy," she said, laughing. "It's nice to think it's just the two of us in the world, at least for a little while."

"Oh, I agree," he said. "I was just hoping you would be on the same page for that."

"We appear to be on the same page for a lot of stuff," she said, "but it's not always quite so simple."

"It never is. It seems like the more you get to know somebody, the more layers you peel back. And then, as you peel them back, you have to figure out who that person is underneath."

"Or you don't have to figure it out," she said, "and you just relax and let things happen as they're meant to happen."

"Yeah," he said. "I was always a doer in life."

"Interesting," she said, "because I'm the same. But you have to consider that, right now, while you're doing what you're doing, you're not a doer, but you're somebody who's letting the world happen."

"Well, when I first arrived, I was letting the world happen," he corrected. "But since I've been here, and definitely now that I've seen the progress, I've gone back to being a doer again."

"Good," she said, as she headed back out again. "I'll talk to you later."

"Can we have a meal together?" he asked.

She stopped and looked at him in surprise. "Sure. Which

one?"

He laughed at that. "I guess you're busy at mealtimes though, aren't you?"

"Well, I am, and I'm not," she said. "I'm always crazy busy up until lunchtime, but, once we start serving, usually it calms down fairly well in the kitchen."

"Lunch," he said instantly. Then he stopped.

"Not a good time?"

"Potentially," he said. "I just don't know if it'll be a bad morning for me, therapy-wise."

"Well, how about this? If you show up, you show up, and, if you don't show up, I'll take that to mean you're in bed. And we'll see how it goes on another day. No pressure. We have time."

"I can deal with that," he said.

"I'll look forward to it." As she walked back into her kitchen, she realized that it was almost a date. She shook her head at that. "A date?"

"What's this? You've got a date?" Gerard asked beside her.

She rolled her eyes at him. "No, I didn't say that." She laughed.

"It'd be good if you had," he said. "It's been a long time for you."

"How would you know?" she teased. "The last time I went out on a date, I wasn't working with you, so you wouldn't even know when it was."

"Oh, we would know now," he said, "because everybody here would be watching you primp and get ready for it."

She smiled a secret smile because, of course, there wasn't a whole lot of that to be had today or here. And that made something about this experience very different. She'd always gone out with healthy able-bodied males. Not that Keith wasn't, but he definitely wasn't as healthy as he could be yet. She could still see the pain in his eyes, the creases around the corners of his eyes and sometimes around his lips when she saw him. It's obvious that he was doing better, but he was a long way from being fully on his feet. Yet should be there in a matter of months. Amazing.

Still, his mental outlook seemed to be improving with his physical progress. That was a plus on both fronts. And those guys from before, the healthy able-bodied males? She always ended up disappointed with their mind-sets or just their lack of plain ethics. And the peeling-back-the-onion reference from earlier? Those walls? Both just seemed to hide ugly aspects that she couldn't handle.

So it didn't bother her in the least to have things start out differently with Keith. It seemed to be a sign of better things to come. So there would be no primping today. Just showing up as who she was. Which was never a bad thing, and she certainly didn't need to dress up to have lunch with him in the middle of her workday.

As she wandered back into her office to take care of a stack of paperwork, her mind kept cataloging the differences between lunch with Keith today versus going out for lunch. But a relationship that started here at Hathaway House started without all that physical attraction. It started with getting to know the person on the inside because the outside appeared to be so broken. She couldn't help but realize just how important that difference was.

Maybe that's why the relationships she'd heard about here were doing so well because they got rid of the outside layers that were often something you couldn't trust, or that weren't even so much about trust but because people weren't necessarily who they really were on the outside. Whereas, in a place like this, who a person really was, was evident every day. The good, the bad, and the ugly. She had yet to see much of the ugly in Keith's case. But she also understood that it was there and that he was working on it. You couldn't ask anybody for more than that.

WELL, KEITH HAD done it. He hadn't really expected to ask her, but it had come out naturally. And casually. Almost like his lunch date was just a request between two friends. He knew it was more. He wanted it to be much more. Something was so special about her, yet it was really hard for him to acknowledge that she would want him. And he knew everybody else would just get plain angry over that. He understood, but it didn't change anything, because really, so much was going on in his world that it was hard to segregate one from the other. Also sad but a fact of life.

Still, he had his morning to get through and more therapy to attend and then his shrink visit, which he absolutely detested. And he knew that they weren't supposed to call them shrink visits, but it was almost like, by insulting the profession, it made it easier to deal with the fact that he had to see her. By the time he was done with his morning physical therapy sessions, he was exhausted already. He managed a shower and then slowly rolled himself toward the psychologist's office. As he entered, she looked at him and smiled.

"Looking a little tired today."

"I'm tired every day," he said. "They don't let you slack down there."

"Do you resent that?"

He groaned. "Why does every question have to have more questions?"

"Fine," she said, "what do you want to talk about?"

He just glared at her.

She smiled and said, "Okay, so how is it to have your sister around?"

"It's nice," he admitted, happy with a question he could at least answer. "I haven't had a whole lot of time to be with her in the last ten years. So this is a really nice opportunity to get to know her again."

"And are you?"

"Am I what?"

"Getting to know her better."

"I just said so," he said. He watched the smile at the corner of the doctor's lips. "Yes, I'm enjoying getting to know her better."

"Good," she said. "She must have a different perspective on the healing here because she comes from working with animals."

"I'm sure she'd say the animals are a whole lot easier than the humans. She doesn't have to tell them to stretch. They do it instinctively. She doesn't have to tell them to rest and to sleep. That's generally what they do. And she doesn't have to sit there and explain everything ten times over to make sure the animals understand what's happening. They don't understand, and she can't explain it to them. The only thing she can do is give them comfort."

"You like that system?"

"I like it better than people who just talk and talk and talk, with their suppositions and theories, their proposals and possibilities," he said. "I would much rather have people just be quiet, show me the work I have to do, and let me get at it."

"Again, very interesting."

He groaned. "Not really," he said. "It's quite simple. I just want to be here for the time I need to be here and then move on."

"And not make any friends in the meantime?"

"I've made friends," he said.

"I've heard," she said.

He frowned at her. "Heard what?"

"That you've been making some friends," she said.

He just shrugged and didn't say anything. No way would he bring up his relationship with Ilse.

"Are you making more than one or just sticking to the one?"

"I haven't really spent too much time getting to know very many."

"Because it's not worth your effort?"

"No," he said. "But it takes time, energy, and effort on their part too."

"Meaning that it's not worth your time," she reiterated.

"Meaning," he stressed, "that there's X amount of time, effort, and energy, and it's all going into my healing."

She leaned back at that, nodded, and said, "That's a good answer."

"Record it then," he said, crossing his arms over his chest.

She studied his body position, and he knew that he would get nailed for the aggressiveness burning inside him.

"So, what is it that you didn't want to talk about?"

"Well, if I wanted to not talk about it, I'm obviously not bringing it up, am I?"

"Tell me about your family."

He stiffened. "Not a whole lot to tell," he said coolly. "My mother died early. My father found a new family, and him and I didn't get along."

"That's often the way of it after a death," she said.

"Well, he certainly didn't wait too long, and he was of no help at all after my mother passed away," he said. "He was drunk, barhopping and sleeping around as much as anybody could possibly manage to fit into those nights," he said in a hard voice. "He threw me out of the house at sixteen. I haven't been back, haven't looked back, and have no interest in talking to him."

He winced at that because he had been wondering if it was something he needed to do, but apparently he was still hanging on to a lot of anger and aggression over it all.

"Sometimes people grow up, and they forgive others," she said. "Other times, people grow up, and they want nothing to do with those people because they don't have the time, the energy, and the effort to put into it," she said, repeating his words. "Your job right now is to look after you."

Surprised that she had echoed his earlier concerns, he nodded quietly.

"However, if you feel like you need to open that door down the road," she said, "pick a time when you're a little more emotionally secure because restarting a relationship like that can be very traumatic."

"Which is why I don't feel like I need to do it now for sure," he said.

"Understandable," she said, "and also a little more difficult because your sister is here."

"Maybe," he said. "I haven't talked to her about it."

"She might help you navigate through some of it, either for or against a conversation with your father."

"She doesn't have a whole lot of interest in reopening that relationship either," he said. "We were both devastated by the way he handled his life back then."

"Has he reached out to you recently?"

Regretfully, he nodded.

"Any particular catalyst in his world to bring that on at this particular time?"

"Yes," he said. "He's getting divorced, realizing that he lost his first family and is now likely to lose his second."

"That'll make a man rethink his current state of affairs," she said.

"He didn't have to do what he did," he said. "He sent us away, cut us out of his life, and made it obvious that we didn't count."

"That's where some of your bitterness and sense of needing to achieve becoming someone is stemming from," she said, with a nod of her head.

He shrugged. "It's every man's dream to grow up and to become a better man than their father. In my case, I didn't have to grow up and try very hard for that. My father wasn't much of a father."

"You're blessed to have a sister you love and who loves you."

At that, he smiled. "Yeah, somehow she turned out to be a beautiful person."

"She does appear to have a good heart," the doc said.

"Yes, and, even though I keep closing doors in her face, and I'm much less of a brother for her than I should be, she keeps sticking by me," he said, and he could hear the note of curiosity in his voice, almost his disbelief as to why she bothered trying.

"Just because your father didn't seem to want you," she said, "it doesn't mean the rest of the world doesn't want you."

"Usually it does," he said. "Too often, people are all about following the same patterns."

"Isn't it more or less the patterns that you set, as you send out that energy of awareness that says, 'Hey, I'm good enough,' or 'I don't like people. Stay away.' Am I right?"

He shrugged. "I don't know," he said. "When I was in active service, I was busy all the time. I had friends. I had a purpose in life. Since the injury, well ..." He turned to look out the window because, since the accident, his only purpose was to get back on his feet. He needed to think further than that now.

For the first time he held out just that little bit of hope that maybe he would get back on his feet. And then what? If that goal was definitely achievable, then he needed to have a goal beyond it. No point in having a goal to get back on his feet if he didn't know how he would live and survive past it.

"What about skills to take into the workforce?"

"Not sure I have too many," he said. "Granted, I have all kinds of skills, but they're not exactly the kind that transfer easily to the private sector."

"Security?"

He shrugged. "That's possible."

"Anything else?"

"I was really good at cybersecurity," he said. "Now, in a perfect world, I'd have a job helping banks work on their cybersecurity."

"Why just banks?" she asked. "In this day and age, anybody who's got a heads-up on keeping corporate clients safe could have a full-time job with a business of their own."

He looked interested for a moment and then shrugged. "It takes capital to start up something like that. I don't have any background in business, and it's not like I'll have any investors give me a year's wages so I can go do that. Beyond that, I don't have any idea who I would even begin to contact for prospective clients, much less convince them that I could do anything to help them out."

She laughed. "I'm pretty sure there was a movie about that many years back. Some thief broke into a bank, just to prove to them that they needed his skills to stop people like him."

"Well, that would be a good way to get me thrown in jail," he said. "So it's not exactly an optimum way to function or to break into the business."

"No," she said, "obviously it isn't. But that doesn't mean it's impossible."

He shrugged. "I don't know. I'll see. Right now, I just have to look after me."

"Oh, I agree," she said. With that, she looked at her watch and said, "Now that wasn't too painful, was it?"

He looked up at the clock behind her head. "Is our session over?"

"Almost," she said. "How are you sleeping these days?"

"I'm sleeping okay. I just wake up early every morning."

"I love early mornings," she said. "It makes my day a lot nicer if I get a few minutes to myself before the world wakes up."

He thought about that and nodded. "Yes, I can agree with that."

After scheduling his next session, he wheeled his way out her office and down to his room.

He thought about his time with the doctor. Something seemed better about the talk with her today. It didn't feel like prying; it wasn't getting under his skin, and it actually seemed helpful. Maybe because she was on his side, and he was looking to justify his position about not contacting his father. It was hard to know what the right answer was, but what he didn't want to do was get pinned into feeling like he had to. He didn't want to feel guilty about everything in life, and too often that was how these relationships made him feel.

As he sat on his bed, waiting for lunch to meet Ilse, his sister called. "Hey, sis. How you doing?"

"I'm okay," she said, "but I was calling to check on you."

"I'm doing okay," he said.

"Did you hear from Dad?" Her tone was abrupt, almost hard.

"Yeah, I did," he said. "Why?"

"Because he's hassling me because you didn't answer him."

"Ignore him," he said. "I'll answer him if and when I feel like it. In the meantime, I don't feel like it."

She gave a broken laugh. "That's you all the time."

"You need to get out of the middle of this," he said gently. "There's no need for it."

"I know," she replied, "but I don't know how to avoid it."

"Tell him to talk to me directly and to stop putting you in the middle," he said. "We aren't children anymore, and we'll do what we want."

"I hear you," she said. "Maybe that's the best answer, after all."

"It is."

"I'm going into town later today. Is there anything you need?"

"Oh," he said, "I hadn't thought about it. This place really does take care of most everything."

"I know," she said, "but I could get you a book or some magazines or whatever you want."

"I think I'm okay," he said. "I'll think about it though. Maybe I'll be ready for you next time."

"Good enough," she said.

After he hung up, he laid back down again and wondered if he wanted anything from town. He wondered why she was going and then realized it was probably all about Iain. He quickly sent her a text. **Feel free to bring Iain back. I'd love to meet him.**

A happy face emoji was the response he got. Then she texted him back. **Someday.**

He wasn't sure why not today, but everybody seemed to have plans of their own. Unfortunately, even when he made plans, they didn't always work out, as, by the time he recovered from his morning physio, lunch was over.

Chapter 10

SEVERAL DAYS LATER Ilse was outside, talking to one of the delivery guys about the temperature of the milk he'd just delivered. It wasn't as cold as it should have been. She happened to glance around and saw Keith walking across the parking lot, using his crutches. She stopped and stared, amazed to see him as mobile as he was, and she was drawn to the intent expression on his face.

"So, is that everything then?" the delivery driver asked impatiently.

She nodded. "For the moment." She signed the bottom of the paperwork, handed it off, then turned and walked across to where Keith was heading. "Hey, it's great to see you up and walking so fast," she called out.

He looked back at her and smiled. "I just wanted a bit of fresh air, and, while I was out here, I just started to feel *right*," he said, with a half shrug. "And, when so much of the world feels wrong, I decided to just follow my instincts and walk a bit."

"You were moving really fast," she said. "It's really great to see."

He smiled and nodded. "It feels really good too."

She looked down at her watch and asked, "Did you get lunch?"

"Not yet," he said. "I was waiting for the crowd to die

down."

"Right," she said, glancing back at the crates that had been just unloaded and were now being moved inside.

"Delivery day?" he asked.

"It seems like every day is delivery day," she said, "but today was dairy, yes."

"Ah, the all-important milk," he said.

"If you were drinking the milk, like you're supposed to be for your bones," she said, "you'd understand."

"Most milk doesn't get along with my stomach," he said. "Sorry."

"It doesn't matter to me," she said, "as long as you're healthy and eating properly."

"Well, I'm certainly eating," he said. "The *properly* part I don't know about. You guys sure put out a ton of food every day though."

"We try," she said. "Is there any particular dish that you're missing?"

He looked at her in surprise. "Fish and chips," he said instantly.

She stared at him and chuckled at his quick response. "Well, I'm glad I asked then," she said. "That's easy enough to do."

"Is it? For this many people?"

"Well, we'll do what we can, and, if we run out, plenty of other food is there," she said comfortably.

He nodded. "So, when can we have it?" he asked, as he wiggled his eyebrows at her.

"Give me at least two days," she said, laughing. "I have to check on my whitefish supply."

"I would think you probably keep that stocked pretty heavily," he said. "Seems like there's fish or seafood of some kind most every day."

"There is," she said, "but I mix it up. And the best fish for fried fish isn't the same kind I use for steamed or baked."

"You're the chef," he said. "I have no idea."

Just then he took a step, and it must have twisted his back wrong. He froze and gasped at the pain, which bleached the color from his face. She wanted to reach out and help him but instinctively knew that would be the wrong reaction. "Just take a few minutes to breathe," she said, her tone calm and controlled. "Everything will be better in a minute."

He groaned. "Who told you that lie?"

She chuckled. "Sometimes we just move too quickly in the wrong direction, and then we pay for it."

"Which is exactly what I just did," he said. Using his crutches, he moved over a few steps closer to the building. "I'll just sit here for a minute." He put the crutches to the side and slowly lowered himself to the top of the waist-high stone wall.

She came over and sat beside him. "It's nice enough out to just sit here anyway," she said, turning her face up to the sun.

"I should have brought something to drink with me," he said.

"Tell me what you want," she said. "I'll go into the kitchen and get it."

He stared at her in surprise, looked at the big open doors to the side, and nodded. "I wasn't even thinking, but it makes sense that you'd have delivery trucks come in right by the kitchen area."

"That's our warehouse room where we keep our stores," she said. "Plus we have walk-in coolers and freezers."

"Could I get some juice and even some water?" he asked.

She hopped to her feet. "Perfect. I'll be back in five." She walked toward the kitchen. Everybody must have intentionally ignored her as she walked through. She just shrugged and didn't say anything and headed to the fridge. Pulling out two cold bottles of water and a cold bottle of juice, she turned and walked back out again. Complete silence followed her.

Once outside, she handed him one of each. Popping the cap off the juice, he took a big long drink. When he was done, he smiled. "Somehow that makes everything seem so much better."

"Now, chase that down with water," she instructed.

"You worried about my blood sugar?"

"Only if you tell me there's a reason to be worried about your blood sugar," she said, studying him carefully. "Is there?"

He laughed. "Nope. No blood sugar issues."

"That's good," she said, "because your diet would need to change if there were."

"I know. No sweets, minimal carbs, and definitely no refined carbs."

"And up the protein and veggies," she said.

He drained half the bottle of water and then relaxed enough to sit back with a happy sigh. "It's really nice out here," he said. "I know it's a parking lot with traffic coming and going, but, because we're a little bit elevated, it gives us a nice view of the whole pasture area and the animals." He pointed out the horses. "I have yet to ask anybody about those."

"Generally they're Dani's horses, but she also brings in a few rescues to be helped out. That's how the llama, Lovely, got here. Seems it was really good friends with the Appaloosa down there, who goes by Appie, by the way. The two came together."

"Well, at least they're here, and they'll have a better life. I have no clue where they were before this," he said, "but I'm sure it wasn't anywhere near as nice as the life they have now."

"I'm certain you're right about that," she said. Laughing, she added, "See that little strawberry-blond filly down there? Somebody was keeping her as an inside pet."

He looked at her in horror.

She nodded and went on. "Obviously she grew too big to be indoors. Her hooves were in really bad shape. It's taken a long time to get them straightened up, but Stan has been working on it."

"I would love to make it down to where my sister works and spend some time with the animals. She brought this monstrous rabbit into my room." He shook his head and laughed about it.

"Hoppers?"

He turned to her. "Yeah. Have you met him?"

"I think everybody has," she said. "She walks him around on a leash quite a bit."

"That's pretty amazing," he said. "She seems happy here."

"Every time I've seen her, she appears to be. She has hardships too, I'm sure. But nobody likes to be in a place where they can't help somebody else."

"True. But, in a place like this, I doubt you get very many deaths."

"It's happened," she admitted. "Not because of something done here but underlying conditions. Still, it's hard to say goodbye when you had such hope and investment in someone's progress."

He winced at that. "I didn't even think of anybody passing away here, but I imagine it's fairly traumatizing for everybody. This is a place of hope, of healing, not walking away or letting go."

"Exactly. But it is what it is. Maybe go hunt your sister up after lunch. If they're busy, they'll tell you," she added thoughtfully. "I've gone down there a few times. Most of the time it's all good, but, once in a while, it's just a nuthouse."

"I'd like to avoid the nuthouse part," he said. "I'm doing okay when I'm out here, but it's not that easy to maneuver if tons of people are there or if I have to navigate among dogs on leashes."

She looked at him thoughtfully. "I can see how that could be a problem. But still, it's well worth going down there. We've all been roped into feeding kittens and looking after injured animals that they've had to keep for a few days to a week. Most of the time it's absolutely delightful, and, of course, it's the middle-of-the-night stuff. They have to handle it anyway, so getting anybody to pitch in really helps."

"I can see that," he said. "You're right. Maybe I should go after lunch." He pulled out his phone and sent his sister a message, while Ilse watched. When the answer came back immediately as a yes, and asking if he wanted her to come and get him, she smiled.

"See? You just have to reach out a little, and asking for help doesn't necessarily have to hurt." With that, she hopped up and said, "I've got to go back inside and return to work."

"Have you had lunch?"

She turned, looked down regretfully, and said, "Yes, I did. But make sure you get yourself something." With that, she headed back inside.

KEITH SADLY WATCHED her go. He had been hoping that maybe she hadn't had lunch. Once he'd seen her with the big delivery truck, he realized that, like everybody else in this place, they all had jobs and responsibilities, something that filled their life outside of physio, shrink visits, and medications. He didn't want to feel like he was useless, but it was definitely a different working path he was on right now.

He didn't want to think about what he would do in the future, but, for the moment, his job was working on himself. But that wasn't her job. Her job was running the kitchens, and it looked to him like she was doing a great job. He'd been hoping she'd see him out here, and of course she had. And their ten-minute visit was great. He'd given her his empty bottles, so he stood up slowly and grabbed his crutches.

Mindful of loose gravel, he made his way to the bottom of the large ramp, which went up to the front reception area. On his first day, he'd been pushed up that ramp in a wheelchair, with someone else pushing, so it had been quite easy to maneuver. He wasn't sure how he would handle it now on crutches, but he was determined to try. He started up slowly, and, about halfway, he got tired.

He wasn't sure what the answer was, but he stopped, rested, and then went a little bit more. He stopped and rested again, and then he went up a little bit more. Before he realized it, he was at the front door. Beaming with the flush of success, he pushed the button to open the door and wandered inside.

One of the girls at the front desk looked up at him and smiled. "Isn't it a beautiful day out there?"

He looked at her and smiled. "It sure is." Tired but happy, he headed down the hallway to his room. He really should go get some food, but he wanted to switch over to the wheelchair. After that climb up the ramp, walking more on crutches was just a little more than he thought he could do.

Back in his room, he grabbed his wheelchair, slowly lowered himself into it, and feeling everything inside just relax, knowing the strain of what he had just done was over, he headed down for lunch. Now that he'd built up an appetite, he couldn't wait to fill up. With any luck maybe he'd meet somebody to have lunch with him.

Even as he had the thought, he had to wonder. Wanting to be around people? Where did that come from? Was it good or bad? As he wandered in, the lineup was gone.

Dennis looked over at him. "Hey, there, are you hungry?"

"Actually, I really am," he said. "What have you got?"

"All kinds of good food," he said. "Come on up here, and let's get you set up."

As soon as Keith had a tray full, he headed out to where he normally sat. It was near the doors, and, when they opened, he loved the fresh air. Shane and a bunch of the other physiotherapists were off to the right, and it looked like another group of staff was having an impromptu meeting at a table just ahead of Keith. He sat down at an empty table, wondering at his choice once again.

Just then, somebody at the table behind him spoke. "Hey, you don't have to sit alone. An empty spot is here, if you want to join us."

He looked at him in surprise, turned to look at the spot,

and said, "Are you sure you don't mind?"

The other guys all smiled. One said, "Join us, please. We've been here so long that we're sick of each other." They all chuckled.

Keith replied, "I haven't been here long enough to know who you are, so it'll be a change for both of us." And, with that, he set down his tray, and, for the first time in a long time, he had lunch with a group of men. Men who understood what he was going through, where he'd been, and what he was heading for. He thought to himself that maybe this was where he belonged.

Chapter 11

THE NEXT FEW days were harried as several of her staff fell ill. Ilse arrived this morning, earlier than normal, more or less running past everything. She didn't get coffee, didn't have a chance to deliver coffee, and by the time the three days were up, she was done. On the fourth morning, she walked in early, not yet knowing if this would be another shorthanded day like the others or not. But, when she walked in, one of her sick men was back to work. She looked at him with joy. "Well, thank heavens you're back, Mike."

He nodded. "Really sorry about being gone. I would have been here if I could have."

"I know," she said, "and we don't want you in here sick anyway. It's best to stay home."

He nodded. "But I'm doing pretty good now," he said. "I've got all the prep started for the breads," he said, "so, if you need to take a few minutes, I've got at least my job covered this morning."

"Well, unfortunately," she said with half a laugh, "you, Tom, and Stefan were out all at the same time."

He looked at her and winced. "Okay," he said. "Well, I'm back doing my job, but I guess we still need to cover for them too, don't we?"

She nodded. "That's why I'm here. I'll get the stock ready, and I have to prep the meat," she said.

"Well, hopefully somebody else will be back in soon too," he said.

"It would be lovely if they were all back today," she said, "but there's no telling when that'll be."

As she prepped the meat, piercing it with little slices and popping garlic cloves into each slit, she put four huge roasts into the oven, so that she had sandwich meat at lunch and also had some leftovers that she needed for other recipes.

With the roasts in the oven on low, she turned her attention to getting breakfast items ready. She had lots of bacon to be laid out, cheese to be sliced, and sausage to be cooked. As she turned around, Stefan walked in too.

She crowed. "Yes! It'll almost seem like it's normal again," she said. "With three of you out, now two back, it'll be like a holiday."

They just laughed at her. "You could take the day off," one of them said.

"Well, if all three of you were back on today," she said, "I might do that, but I really don't trust that just yet."

"Trust what?" they asked, with feigned innocence.

She smiled at them. "Trust that it'll all work out. I want to make sure we've got lots of staff here," she said. "We're behind on our desserts. We even had to cut back to two choices every day."

"I bet nobody noticed either," Stefan said.

"Maybe they didn't," she said, "but I did."

They just nodded because nobody in that kitchen was anywhere near as fanatical as she was when it came to the quantity of what she needed. But that's the way it was, and, with them back at work, she wanted to make sure that everything was ready and that the deliveries were on track. Then she made herself a pot of coffee and grabbed a cup.

When she realized what time it was, she grabbed a second cup and walked to Keith's room. His door was open, and his light was on, but he looked up at her in surprise.

"I wondered what was up with you," he said. "I haven't seen you in days."

She nodded, walked over with two cups in her hands, and placed one for him on the nearby night stand. "I had three guys out sick at once," she said, wiping her fluffy hair off her forehead. "I'll drink this coffee, and then I'm heading back to my place for a couple hours."

"Ouch. Three gone at once sounds pretty rough."

"We all have to pitch in and do the job," she said. "It can just make for a really tough time of it when it goes on that long."

"Yeah, I would think so," he said. "Are they all back now?"

"Well, two are for sure," she said, "and I'm hoping the third one will too, but I haven't seen him yet, since he doesn't normally show up for another hour."

"Perfect," he said. "Sit down and rest a bit."

She smiled with a nod. "That's why I brought two cups with me."

He laughed. "Well, I wondered if you were making up for having missed out on a couple days."

"Well, I was hoping you'd understand that, if I was here, I was here, and, if I wasn't here, it's because I couldn't make it."

"Exactly," he said with a smile.

She studied his face. "You looked pretty well rested."

"I did a bit too much, and we backed off some of the workouts, so, if I'm looking a bit rested, it's because I'm not doing as much now because I overdid it earlier," he confessed.

"Hey, there's worse ways to do something wrong," she said. "It seems like you're quite a bit happier right now though." As a matter of fact, he looked more settled, calmer, and the pain didn't appear to be twisting his insides up the way it was before. He just looked more at peace with himself all the way around.

"I'm feeling better," he said, "and seeing progress that I hadn't really expected to see. I'm not completely out of the weird moodiness, but I am feeling better as I look forward."

"Look forward to what?"

"To whatever comes after this," he said. "For the longest time I could only see this. And now I realize there's so much more."

"There is, indeed," she said, "and I'm glad that you can finally see something after that. What about your sister?"

"Well, I went down to the vet's office," he said with a bright smile. "They had dogs and cats and a huge macaw that was just gorgeous." He smiled and shook his head. "I hadn't realized how colorful my sister's life was."

"Isn't it nice to see what she created for herself?" Ilse said.

"It is, indeed. I've never seen her work, and it's not what I thought. You know? When you think *vet tech*, I figured, surgery, helping the vet, taking temperatures and changing dressings and such, and she does that too, but she also bathes the animals, cleans their cages. It's not what I thought she would be doing, yet she loves every minute of it."

"Well, I think it's a very unusual place here," she said, "not just for the men and women whom we have working there but also because of the vet clinic being here as part of Hathaway House."

"Agreed. I met Racer, and a cat named Thomas," he said with a big smile. "It was just nice to grab a cat and hold it."

"A cat would let you do that?" She shook her head. "I'm more of a dog person but that rabbit? Man, if I had room for him, I'd take him home in a heartbeat."

"He's pretty darn big," Keith said. "If you had a fence, you'd probably be fine. But, if you have a dog around, you've got to make sure it's one that gets along with the rabbit because I'm not sure, if they went toe to toe, who would win the fight."

She chuckled. "You'd always assume the dog would, but those rabbits have pretty vicious back legs."

"This guy's back legs are huge paddles," he said, "so I don't know who would win."

"Exactly." When her coffee was gone, she looked at it regretfully. "I should have brought a flask with me."

"That just makes you sound like a coffee addict," he teased.

"Well, I'm definitely addicted to something," she said. "I just don't know if it's good or bad yet."

And, on that note, she stood, gave him a small wave, a smile, and walked out.

WHAT DID SHE mean, she was addicted to something? Keith racked his brain, with the usual addictions coming to mind. He'd never seen her with an alcoholic drink, but then she was on the clock here. He didn't get the sense that she smoked—even cigarettes—so he doubted she used recreational drugs. She was addicted to coffee, of course, but then so was he. More than that, he was addicted to her visits.

The last few days he'd felt bereft, wondering what was going on with her, but then had heard from Dennis that the kitchen was under siege with so many people out sick, and Keith figured that either she was one of the sick or she was just working constantly, trying to keep up with her kitchen. And that had to be tough, since clearly she was already dedicated, arriving first thing in the morning, staying until everybody else was gone. The fact that she lived on the property and had access to go home and have a midday break helped too, but it said much about her life, that she was here cooking all the time. It appeared that she didn't have a lot of time for a life outside of her work. And that was something he worried about. If he were to leave, how would he maintain a relationship with her if she was always working? Surely chefs typically had morning shifts or evening shifts, didn't they?

He wasn't sure what to think of that. But, as he was spending all his time healing and doing all the work he had to do, she was spending all her time doing the work that she had to do. It's just that he was doing it for himself, and she was doing it for a paycheck. Not that he wanted to undermine her passion and what she was doing because it was obviously very valuable and because she was good at it too. But he did wonder what she would be like if she had a full-time relationship but was so busy all the time at work too.

His morning was slow, but he was off slightly on his sessions with Shane, even though he tried hard to pick it up now that he knew that Ilse was around again. But Shane was frustrated with him.

"What's wrong with you?" he snapped. "I said a hundred percent effort. Not sixty-five and that's all I've seen out of you today."

"No, you're right," he said, rotating his shoulders and easing his head back. "I'm not sure what's wrong with me. I'm just off a bit."

"Well, get back on again," Shane said. "We're done for the day." He waved his hand. "Go home, go for a swim, and work some of that out of there."

Keith nodded and quickly made his way to the wheelchair and left. He didn't like Shane being pissed off at him either. It wasn't a state that he was used to seeing, but Shane was usually trying to get Keith to do his best, and no way was he doing that today. He wasn't even sure what was wrong because he'd been upset before, when he didn't know why Ilse hadn't been around. But he'd found out she was back, so why wasn't he "back" as well?

It was frustrating when you couldn't come up with a reason why something was off. It was just off. Only that wasn't good enough when you were here for however long; you had these people's talents and skills available to help you get from point A to point B. Just because Keith wanted to dawdle somewhere in the middle didn't mean that the staff had the time for it.

Feeling upset at himself, he headed back to his room, where he quickly washed up and changed his T-shirt. He grabbed his crutches and slowly maneuvered his way to the cafeteria. He wasn't even sure that he'd worked up enough of an appetite. Shane had told him to go swimming, but he hadn't realized what time it was. Still, he had on his swim shorts, so he should either go swimming first or he could go later.

When he took one look at the long line in the dining room, he decided he'd eat later, and he took the elevator down and made his way to the pool. Stripping off the T-shirt, he jumped into the water.

As soon as it closed over his head, he could feel some of the stress and the confusion in his world floating away. This is what he needed. Just a chance to veg out and to get down here, not be ordered around, not be told what to do by anybody, and just have the time to do for himself. And what he really wanted to do was just swim, and that's what he did, heading from one side to the other mindlessly. Blindly trying hard to keep his form, he just worked steadily, back and forth.

When he finally broke through the water and eased back to just float, he saw Shane standing there, looking down at him. "Problem?" he asked.

"No," Shane said, "not at all. Just glad to see you put more effort into that than you did upstairs."

"Sorry," he said. "I don't know what's wrong with me."

"Woman trouble?" Shane asked, his hands on his hips, frowning at him.

"Actually not," he said. "I was worried because she hadn't shown up for a few days, but she was there this morning."

"Well, I know the last couple days she's been slammed in the kitchen," he said, "because some of the staff members were out sick."

"I knew that," he said, "because she came today."

"Good," Shane said, "but after all that I didn't get anything close to your best efforts, so having her show up again obviously didn't affect things much."

"It didn't. You're right," he said. "It just reminds me that, although life is changing, it's not necessarily changing enough."

"Explain," he barked.

"I can't really explain it, but, even if I wanted to have a relationship with somebody, that somebody is here working all the time," he said. "I can't stay here forever obviously, so I'm not sure what solution there is."

"Well, you're not going anywhere soon," he said. "I wouldn't want to see you leave here for at least another two months."

He stared at him in surprise. "Do you think I need to be here that much longer?"

"Absolutely," Shane said. "You've come a long way, but it's just the beginning to get you where you need to be."

Keith nodded slowly. "Okay," he said, "I was thinking I would only be here for another couple weeks."

"I would say eight at the minimum," Shane said. "It could be closer to twelve if not sixteen. Even once we get you back up to peak performance," he said, "we have to stabilize all those muscles in that spinal column of yours. We'll be a long time at it, so spend the time getting to know and to enjoy her. If it's something that you want to keep up when you're done and you're healthy," he said, "you'll find a way. Don't start making problems ahead of time."

At that, Shane turned and walked away. He stopped at the bottom of the stairs, going up to the dining room deck, and said, "And, hey, don't do so much swimming that you don't eat."

"Yes, boss," Keith said and then laughed. He hadn't wanted to come to Hathaway House and, even when he'd arrived, he didn't want to stay. Now he couldn't stop laughing because he could stay for at least another two to four months. And that was perfect. How far he had come was evidenced by that alone.

Chapter 12

ILSE DID TAKE two days off. She really needed them. She was completely burned out, and her crew, now that they were back up and running fully staffed, had everything in hand. She went into town and visited friends, saw a movie, and did some shopping. By the time she came back to work two days later, she couldn't wait to see if Keith was awake. When she walked into his room, he looked up and laughed.

"This time I asked Dennis, and he said you were off for a couple days."

She nodded. "Exactly," she said, "I don't take enough time off as it is. I did mention it before I left."

"I know. It just seemed longer. I was wondering how that worked," he said. "In case I ever get out of this place, and we wanted to spend some time together," he said, waggling his eyebrows, "how do you make time for that when you're always here working?"

"I'm here a lot because I don't have any other life," she said, laughing. "This has been my whole life for a long time now."

"When was your last relationship?" he asked.

"Years ago," she said. "I've dated since then, but I haven't met anybody who I really cared about."

"Until now," he nudged.

She chuckled. "Until now," she agreed. "And it's hard to

say where you're heading yourself, right?"

"Well, for the first time, I know," he said. "I spoke with Shane about it a couple days ago, and I guess I'm here for a while yet, which was great news."

"Oh, wow," she said. "It's funny though, most people don't want to stay here long-term."

"No," he said. "And that's where the problem comes in because, as soon as I do leave, I don't know how to keep in touch with you."

"Well, I'm sure we can …" Just then her cell phone beeped. She hopped to her feet. "Looks like I've got to go." And, like that, she was gone.

AND HE HAD to wonder. Was she just a workaholic? Maybe this was also her way of getting away from having an intimate or personal conversation. He had no way to know exactly what they were to each other at this point. It was funny, but they were bouncing off it, coming together and bouncing off, almost like the beginning stages of a real relationship. It was real in every other way, except that he couldn't exactly take her on a date. They couldn't go see a game or take a walk in the park together. But then he hadn't been all that successful in his other relationships, going to a game, taking a walk, having dates. And this had started here with even less. But, then again, without all the usual societal details of typical dating, they were focused on something more important.

They were each getting to know the other, the real person on the inside. All the rest of it was just window dressing. He laughed at that because it was one thing to feel that way when you had a healthy, strong, or physically fit body. But it was another thing entirely when every muscle and bone had been damaged. He knew that any storm that came now would make his bones ache something fierce. But she would understand that as well.

He knew that things between them had gone deeper and faster than in most cases or in a normal relationship because, when you dated, you kept things on a superficial level. You went dancing. You went to the movies and did various things like that. He just wasn't sure if that was good or bad. After you got through that first flush, it was easy to see that there were issues still. No matter where they lived, there would have to be some meeting of the minds over various issues. And that would be true no matter what relationship he had.

Somebody would have to get used to his physical issues, just the same as he would have to get used to somebody else's issues. For instance, in her case, her workaholic tendencies. And that was fine. Life was all about making adjustments. But it still felt odd, like he wasn't quite home and wasn't quite ready to go in that direction. He didn't know what was holding him back because he'd made such progress in so many different ways. But he had to admit a little bit of fear resided in the back of his mind. He decided that, when he went for his next shrink appointment, he'd just bring it up.

And when he did, the doctor looked at him and asked, "What is it you think is holding you back?"

"I don't know," he said, "it just seems—I don't know." And he couldn't fill it in with words. He had gotten a whole lot more comfortable talking with her. As shrinks went, she was okay. She never pressed or pushed, but she had a gently insistent way of asking questions over and over again.

"That you're not quite whole, maybe?"

"Maybe," he said, "but it feels like it's something else."

"How about trust?"

He looked at her and winced. "In what way?"

"What way is there?" she asked slowly.

"I don't know," he said in frustration. "That's why I brought it up."

"And I like that," she said. "I really like that. It makes a huge difference if you're willing to look into your own treatment and truly participate."

"Maybe," he said, "but it still feels like something else is there."

"Do you think it goes back to your father?"

Something inside him stilled. "I hope not," he said harshly. "I really don't want to open that door."

"And yet," she said slowly, her gaze direct, "have you ever been in love? Have you ever been married? Have you ever had a relationship where you wanted it to be *the one*?"

"I've been in love," he said, "but I've never been married."

"Why not?" she asked.

He took a deep breath and then let it out slowly. "My girlfriend said that I was afraid of committing."

"Interesting," the doctor said. "And that would fit."

"Fit in what way?" he asked, bewildered. "How would anybody even know that?"

"Think about your father, the person who, besides your mother, was supposed to be there for you. To care for and to nurture children abandoned by their mother."

"Stop," he said. "I wasn't abandoned. She died."

"That's true, but, despite the circumstances, many times we feel that we've been abandoned when somebody in our life has died," she corrected him gently. "You're still the child who was left behind when she left without you."

"But she didn't want to," he said rather desperately, feeling something tweak inside himself.

"Of course not," she said with a gentle smile. "That's a given. But it doesn't mean that, deep down, that little boy didn't feel like you were supposed to go with her. Or that your life would have been forever different if she hadn't left you."

"That's true," he said.

"Then we come to your father," she said. "Somebody you're still very angry with, over his treatment of you. And he's dared to come back into your life to try to create a relationship in order to make himself feel better, when, as far as you're concerned, that relationship's already long been dead, done, and over with."

He just stared at her. "How did you figure all that out?"

"My job is to understand people," she said gently. "And really? You're not any different than the others. We all have hurts. We all are works in progress."

"Ouch," he said. "I was thinking I was very different."

"When you arrived, you didn't care what happened," she said. "You were morose, brooding, and moody," she said. "But why?"

"I don't know," he said. "I just didn't care."

"Why didn't you care?"

"Because—" and he stopped. He sank back in the chair. "I don't know."

"That's fine," she said, "but I want you to think about it over the next few days and see what answer might rise to the surface."

"What if no answer rises?" he asked bitterly. "I came *here* to get answers."

"I don't have answers for you," she said in surprise. "You're the one with the answers."

"But what if I don't have this answer?" he asked.

"Then you're not looking in the right place."

Chapter 13

IT WAS AN odd thing to realize, when she had coffee with Keith, just how addicted she was to being in his presence. And just how much she wanted to be with him. How much she wanted to take this relationship to the next level. Whatever that meant. And so, when he spoke about leaving, her heart just surged.

Of course he would leave at some point. She too was grateful that it wouldn't be anytime soon, but she could also see he'd been thinking about it. And so he should. This wasn't just his life; this *was* her life. But it didn't have to be quite so crazy of a life. She was the one who had made it that way. But the thought of him leaving left a great big gaping hole in her heart.

She'd been off now for a couple days. Mentally off and physically off. She had worked hard to hide it, but it was obvious by the looks of everybody around her that they were walking on tiptoes, trying to figure out just what was going on. She didn't have an answer for them. It seemed like she didn't have any answers for anybody these days, and that was apparently how Keith felt too.

She didn't see a shrink. She didn't go through therapy or any of the other million treatments that they went through here. She was just the person who provided food. But she could see how much the food meant to the staff but mostly to the patients, when she saw their progress throughout the weeks. But she also saw men come and men go, and maybe that's why she had avoided relationships here and elsewhere—because she didn't like the leaving part.

It felt wrong to get involved with somebody only to say goodbye. As she stared down at her hands, holding the great big bowl of dough in front of her, she realized she didn't want to say goodbye. That was the difference this time. She really didn't want to say goodbye. So, in a way, she wished she hadn't even said hello. But it was too late for that. She couldn't put this genie back in the bottle, and it was definitely something she would have to find a way to work around. Relationships work for all kinds of people, in all kinds of ways. She just had to find what would work for them.

The trouble was, she didn't even know where he lived permanently. People came here from all across the country. If he would be local, that was a whole different story, but, if he was returning to somewhere else, she wasn't sure what she was supposed to do. And, because of that, it seemed like everything she did had a little extra snap to her wrist or a little extra bite to her voice.

She didn't mean it that way; she was just dealing with the fact that she didn't have any answers, and she was frustrated. And that completely sucked. She went through a couple more days of seeing him in the morning but then being busy during the day, as she tried to work her way through this personal dilemma of hers. And still, she didn't find any answers. Finally, at noon one day, she looked up to see Dennis staring at her. "What's the matter?"

"That's my line," he said with a smile. "What's the matter with you?"

"I didn't think anything *was* the matter," she said cautiously.

"You probably should just sit down and talk with him."

"What makes you think I need to talk with him?"

"Because the only things that can twist a person into a pretzel and spit you out like this, not even whole," he said, "are relationships."

She winced at that. "Is it that obvious?"

"Not really," he said, "but I know you pretty well. I also happen to think that you and Keith are a great match."

"Most people wouldn't agree with you," she said, fascinated.

"Doesn't matter what most people think," he said. "The only ones in this relationship are the two of you, and you two are all that matter."

"Well, that's true enough," she said, "but you know how I never get involved because people come and go all the time."

"Yeah," he said. "You said you aren't into short-term relationships. That you're an all-or-nothing gal."

"When he started talking about leaving," she said, looking down at the bowl in her hands again, "it just hit me that I'd done exactly what I said I would never do. I would never get involved in a short-term relationship."

"How do you know it's a short-term relationship?" he asked.

She looked up at him. "He's not necessarily talking about staying close by. Like all of them, he'll leave here."

"Maybe so but his sister is here," he said. "You're forgetting that."

She looked at him in surprise, and then a delighted grin split her face. "You know something? I did forget. So … I guess, even if he does leave the center, he's not necessarily breaking off all contact with his sister, is he?"

Dennis laughed. "You see? Normally you're a smart, intelligent woman, but I've seen other smart people break down and become needy, pathetic, completely uncertain—simply because of a failure to sit down and to work things out with their partner."

"I know," she said. "Relationships make me all wobbly and unsure of myself."

"Exactly. If you're worried about what to do from here," he said, "then I suggest you talk to him."

"I just don't want to add to his stress," she said. "He's under a lot of pressure already."

"News flash. Relationships are pressure. They are stress. There isn't any easy answer for anybody," he said. "So go get the answers that you need now, and then you have something to work forward from. Without the answers, all you'll end up doing is stewing for nothing and spinning around in circles."

She looked at him in surprise. "When did you get to be so smart?"

"I was born this way." And, with a chuckling laugh, he turned and walked out again.

But he was right. All her nerves and worries were because she hadn't sat down and talked with Keith. And that was something she aimed to fix. She smiled. She'd have to do something special, but what?

HIS FATHER'S EMAIL burned away at the back of his brain. Keith wasn't ready to open that can of worms, but he couldn't stop himself from feeling like he should. He did need to make sure that Robin was out of the middle and that he was moving forward with his life. After what seemed like an interminable amount of time, where he'd made no progress at all, he was now making progress by leaps and bounds. The fact that every morning he woke up early, waiting and hoping Ilse would walk in the door, said so much about his mental state. But more than that, he also knew that she liked him and that they were building something together. Something he hadn't expected. He had deliberately shied away from relationships all his life, not only because of his work but because of his father.

His sister was his only healthy relationship, and that didn't say a whole lot about him. On the other hand, Keith was prepared to learn and to grow and to move on in reclaiming his life and his health. Anything to keep Ilse at his side. That brought up something else, as in what he would do for a job. He remembered the suggestions from the discussion with his shrink before and wondered about it. He could also ask somebody else in his condition about what kind of issues there were in this transition from naval life to civilian life, in this transition from his first career to his second one.

As he pondered it all, a knock came on his door, and a tall stranger walked in. Keith looked up with a nod and said, "Good morning."

The man walked forward, reached out a hand, and said, "I'm Iain."

He stared at him in surprise. "Robin didn't tell me that you were coming."

"I didn't tell her," he said easily. "I know she's worried about your reaction to me."

Keith smiled and shook his head. "Robin has always

been a force unto herself. She will do whatever she thinks is right, but, at the same time, she'll worry in the background."

Iain grinned. "Isn't that the truth?" He looked at Keith. "I didn't know what time was good to catch you."

"Right now isn't bad," Keith said. "I just came back from getting coffee, and it's not quite breakfast time yet. You're here pretty early, aren't you?"

"I am," he said. "I came to do a bit of carpentry work downstairs at the vet clinic for Robin and Stan."

"Good. It's got to feel pretty decent to be in a position where you can do that now." He frowned as he noted the huge envelope Iain held up now.

"I brought these for you," he said. "Not that you'll care necessarily, but I thought I'd give it a try."

Keith pulled some pictures out. The first was of Iain when he'd arrived. Keith recognized a lot of similar things in the photo of Iain as compared to Keith's own photos, but the most profound element was the look on Iain's face. Like Robin had told Keith, Iain had been here—depressed, down, almost surly, and looking at the world as if nothing would ever change. Keith barely even commented on Iain's physical body. "Man, that face," Keith said. "I so recognize that look."

"Right," Iain said. "I was such an idiot for the way I traveled here." He shook his head as he stared down at the man that he had been. "I was in such a narrow mind-set, and I couldn't see beyond it. We get locked up with all our pain, our depression, and our emotions that are just not quite clear, and it's painful to look back on it now."

As Iain reached for another photo, Keith was still struck by the fact that the man standing before him was the complete antithesis of the man in the first photo. Keith didn't even really need to see the next photo, but, when he did, he saw not just the pride on Iain's face but also the muscle growth, the development, the calming down of some of the angry muscle tissue, the vibrancy of his spirit. Keith looked up at the man in front of him. "I can see why you hang on to these photos."

"Nobody ever believes me," Iain said, pulling up a chair with a grin. With a single hand, he flipped it around and sat down casually, a man who was once again in control of his body.

"I'm not there yet," Keith said boldly.

"You haven't been here long enough," Iain said. "You'll need months, depending on the damage. Sometimes the surgeries are the easiest, but it's the muscle rebuilding that takes the longest."

"That's what I'm finding," Keith said with a wince. "Just when you think you get progress, you also have a setback."

Iain's booming laughter rang across the room. "It can, indeed. Of all the stages of life I'm glad to have over with, it was leaving here. Don't get me wrong. This is the best place to be for rehab, for recovery, for success. And I owe everything to my time here. It gave me a life back. Some of the staff are really tough, and they make you work but, when they do, wow."

"Are you talking about Shane by any chance?" Keith asked with a smirk.

"Oh, yeah. I've screamed at him and cried with him. You know when you get to that breaking point, and there's nothing else left? Shane would say that's when the real Iain showed up."

"Yes, I've been there," Keith said. "It hasn't been as dramatic as yours, but I've certainly been in a position where

I could see that I had to work harder, be more, and do something to show the improvements, and I'm almost there now."

Iain looked at him and smiled a knowing smile. "You're not even close," he said. "I remember this stage. It was about halfway through." He pointed to his legs. "It's so much farther than you ever thought you'd get, so you think it's good. It's good enough. You think that maybe you can live with this because you're afraid to hope for more.

"But I'm here to tell you that there is so much more, and you have to give them a chance to give it to you. I've seen guys walk away early because they couldn't stand being away from their families so long. And sure, their rehab could continue at another place, but it's not the same. Every day you get here is a gift. You need to make as much use of it as you can, and, when you're lucky enough to get the full benefit, you end up with something like I did." He smiled. "Every day I wake up and bounce out of bed, grateful that my body works again."

"I can see that," Keith said, and he could, but Iain was so far advanced from where Keith was that it was hard to see himself there.

Iain smiled, nodded, and said, "Listen. I know what you're thinking because I felt it too. I saw other people, who were way ahead of me, and I knew it couldn't possibly be the same for me. But I was wrong, very wrong, and so are you. Even if you're upset and worried right now, just know that you have a lot of room for more progress, and it's worth every bead of sweat." Then he grinned. "And, by the way, I'm going to marry your sister," he said. "Some would say I should be asking for your permission, but, since I'm not doing that, no matter how you feel, asking seemed insincere."

The change in conversation caught Keith off guard. He looked at Iain, smiled slowly, and said, "Well, I'm really glad to hear that," he said, reaching out for a handshake, "because she is head over heels in love with you."

"The feeling is mutual," Iain said with a gentle smile. "She's unlike anybody I've ever met before. And a far cry from the kind of woman I used to go out with."

"We're different men now," Keith said.

"Not only different," he said, "but because of the real relationship it is, and the way it started here at Hathaway House, there's no comparison. In this place, you see people in an honest way, at their worst in some cases, and that has to be dealt with first. It's not like the supposed real world, where everybody has all these layers and layers of fakeness that you have to get through to find out who the person is on the inside. Here, fake doesn't work. Here, it is what it is, and you have to deal with it. The good news is that, by the time you survive the first stages of a transparent relationship, you have something that's solid, and it can go the distance."

"I hear you there," he said. "I've been thinking about those issues myself."

Iain looked at him, his lips quirking. "Have you met someone?"

Keith flushed. "I have," he said, "and believe me. Nobody was more surprised than I was."

"I think that's a standard response for those of us lucky enough to have it happen," he said. "I don't even understand it myself. Robin could have anybody, so why someone all busted up like me? Now that also gave me the impetus to work a little bit harder, to make sure that I came to her as physically sound as I could possibly be. The reality is that, because of all the surgeries and the injuries, things could get a little uglier down the road, but she says she's fully prepared for that. I don't know that I am though," he admitted honestly. "But it is what it is, and, having met Robin, I'm no longer prepared to be alone, and I'm not afraid anymore to commit to me and to her."

His words still impacted Keith, long after Iain had walked away. They would meet again for lunch with his sister, and Keith was thrilled. She'd found somebody who appeared to be a decent guy and somebody Keith could relate to, which was even better. But that last comment about no longer being afraid really stayed with him. Is that what Keith had been doing?

He thought back to the young kid he'd been when his mother had died. He'd been devastated, and then his father's inability to deal with raising two kids alone had been equally difficult. But, when his father had remarried, Keith had been angry and sullen, and for the first time he could really see that his father couldn't handle Keith at all. So it was for the best that Keith had stepped out. As it was, he had moved into a friend's garage apartment, but even that was on the edge of too close to his father, and, after another year or so, he ended up in the navy.

It helped though. It had been enough for him to realize that the world was a great big oyster and that he needed to do something for himself.

Joining the navy had been the absolute best thing he could have done. It made him into a responsible and a highly functioning adult male. He could see that his father was still wallowing, grabbing what happiness he could by remarrying and having a second family, but it appeared he was headed into troubled waters again.

That was his problem though; it wasn't something Keith or Robin could fix. Keith needed to let go of the fear that had crippled his relationships. Fear of losing someone. He'd lost his mother, then his father. All his romantic relationships had sailed along until it came to the commitment part, and then he'd balked because he just knew there was no such thing. There was no *happily ever after.* Craziness happened, including death, divorce, and remarriage. And he didn't want any part of it.

He sagged back into his bed, staring out the window. Something needed to give, and maybe Iain's visit had broken things loose and had brought this on. It was hard to dislike the man. He was friendly, cheerful, and so much further down the path that, instead of being jealous, Keith was inspired. See? Yet another shift in his mind-set. Being inspired wasn't something he was ever used to being. Now he was willing to see somebody ahead of him and to know that amazing progress was possible. He picked up his phone, quickly sent his sister a text. **Just met Iain. Nice guy.**

He really is. See you at lunch—crazy morning.

He put down his phone, once again reminded of the fact that everybody else had a job. Everybody else had their careers figured out—except for him. He should have asked Iain what he was doing with his life because Keith needed a hand figuring out what to do with his. As he sat here, he looked up in surprise to see Iain and Ilse both walking back into his room. She had coffee, and so did Iain.

Iain looked at him, smiled, and said, "I just met this beautiful young friend of Robin's delivering coffee for you," and there was a question in his eyes.

Keith tried to ignore him, looking up at Ilse instead. "And here I wondered if you'd forgotten," he teased.

"As if I could forget," she said. She put down his coffee and said, "I can't stay. I've got to head back to the kitchen. Things are blowing up again."

"And you'll deal with it like you always do," he said comfortably.

She laughed, smiled, and said, "I'll take that vote of confidence today." And, with that, she booked it down the hallway.

Iain looked at him with a big grin on his face. "Not bad. Not bad at all."

"Right?" Keith said, feeling like a little kid. "Sure didn't expect it to happen."

"That is what makes it the best thing ever," he said.

Keith blurted out, "I would ask—" and then broke it off. He didn't really know how to ask Iain, essentially a stranger, such a question. He would become part of the family, but it wasn't the same thing.

"Ask what?" Iain prompted.

"Well, I—I'm trying to figure out what to do when I'm done with my rehab here," he said. "I know that I've got another couple months here, maybe more. But then what?"

Iain nodded but stayed quiet.

"One of the things that I was involved in was cybersecurity," he said. "I was just wondering if you had any clue how one would set up something like that, how to get it started."

Iain's eyebrows shot up. "Oh, that's interesting," he said, "and you're way better off from a skill-set perspective than a lot of guys coming into civilian life from the military."

"I know," he said. "It just happens to be something I had a knack for, so I tended to get put into that side of it a lot."

"The government machine is nothing if not effective at

using your skills."

"Sometimes, but other times they do the stupidest things, and you, with all your skills, find yourself walking around on a foot patrol."

Iain laughed and laughed. "God, isn't that the truth! When I think of the number of times I was put out on a job, then looked at the other guy like, *What are we doing here?*"

"Exactly," Keith said. "I'm not even sure who mentioned it, but somebody suggested I contact local companies or banks or something, to see just what people could use in that area."

"Well, it's certainly timely that you mentioned it," Iain said. "I was in the same boat not that long ago, and, right now, I am in the process of setting up a center for helping guys like yourself get back into the workforce."

"Really?" he said. "So maybe you're the right person to talk to."

"Maybe," he said. "The thing is, I do know a couple guys who have already established their company, and they are in New Mexico. About seven of them, and they do all kinds of jobs."

"Meaning?'

"I'm not quite sure what I'm doing here yet, so maybe I'll talk to them about their journey into this."

"New Mexico, huh?" He pondered the thought. "You're not talking about Badger, are you?"

Iain looked at him in delight. "See? We even have friends in common," he said. "Badger and his entire team had a pretty rough recovery after a bad accident, but now they're well past that stage. They've set up a big center to help vets. They do everything from security to carpentry apparently. They're even involved in K9 work now."

"Well, I don't have any experience in that," he said, "but I have a lot in the cyberattack and cybersecurity realm."

"What about government-level work?"

"I could," he said. "I'm not against it. I could also do covert contracts. I don't have any other people to work with, but it wouldn't hurt to have something just for myself to handle."

"I'll think about it," he said, "and see if I have any connections to pull on."

"Thanks, I'm doing the same."

Iain stayed and visited a little bit longer, then Keith said, "Guess I should get ready for breakfast."

"Yep, I hear you," he said. "I'm waiting for Robin to pop up, and then I'll go back down again with her."

"Good enough," Keith said. "Hey, if you get a chance, stop by again."

"I'm back and forth anyway," Iain said. "I settled in Dallas." He smiled at him. "That's something you may want to consider yourself."

"Why Dallas?" Keith asked, as he swung his legs over the edge of the bed.

"Because of the girlfriend scenario, to be near her," Iain said, then he was gone.

Keith thought about that as he grabbed his crutches and made his way to the kitchen. That was a good thing to remember, and he hadn't even discussed it with Ilse. She might not know what his plans were, but he'd been worried about whether she would have time for him. She had to be considering whether he would be sticking around or not. They really needed to just sit down and talk.

After breakfast he headed to his morning physio session. He was very preoccupied, and Shane was getting pissed again. Finally he sat him down in the chair. "What is with you today?"

He took a deep breath and said, "I just met Iain."

Shane stopped in his tracks. "And?"

"And nothing," he said. "Obviously the change in him is unbelievable, and it must be a huge boon to you guys."

"But—"

"No buts," he said. "I mean, he's done a phenomenal job of improving himself."

"And so would you if you'd pay attention," Shane said in exasperation.

Keith looked up at Shane. "Sorry, man. Just dealing with some eye-opening stuff today."

"I hope so," he said, "because this has to stop. This is a couple days in a row now, and we can't do that."

Keith looked at him in surprise. "Seriously?"

"Seriously," Shane said. "Every day you need to show up prepared to do the job."

"I have," Keith said in protest.

"You have physically," he said, "but not mentally. And that needs to shift."

Next up was his shrink appointment. He walked in, still distracted.

"I hear you're struggling," she said. "What's going on?"

"I had some eye-opening discussions," he said, then told her about Ilse, his relationship with his father, and how he'd always avoided long-term commitments. "I feel I can open that door with Ilse. I think it will be an important step for me down the road. I mean, it takes two to have a working relationship, a successful one. I still need to discuss that with her. I'm willing to look at that commitment step when the time comes. But I have to look after me first."

"Is that the root of your problem with Shane?"

He winced. "You heard about that, huh?"

"We're a team," she said. "Your team. We have to work together."

"I don't know," he said. "I didn't realize I was holding back."

"According to Shane, you're not giving it your all."

Keith stopped. "You know what? It's really irritating to hear that because he's seen so many guys, and it's like there's no way Shane doesn't see what he needs to see in me. And obviously he feels like I'm not giving it everything I've got, but I'm on the other side of that, and it feels like I'm giving him what he's expecting, but it's not enough."

"There's the problem," she said with a gentle smile. "You're giving him what *he* wants. You're not giving him what you want."

He stared at her in surprise. But inside was that kernel of truth. "Are you saying that, in some stupid sick way, I want to stay like this?"

"No, not at all. I'm saying that the little child caught in the nightmare inside you is afraid that, by giving it your all, it still won't be enough. So, if you only give half of your all, you'll always have an excuse for when you fail or for when you don't get the success you had hoped for. You can just say, *You tried, and it didn't work out.* But secretly, you'll be safe because you know you held back, so *you*, the real you, didn't fail."

He winced at that. "God, that sounds terrible."

"And it probably is," she said, "but it doesn't change the reality of what you've got happening here. And now what you need to think about is what's important. Think about what it is you want out of life and whether you're prepared to really reach for it. In this case, I'll say what you're actually reaching for is happiness, something that you've never really had. Not since your mother died."

Chapter 14

ILSE WAS A little distracted herself, as she figured out what was going on in her world, as she wondered how best to let Keith know what was going on between them. But she'd also recognized that he was distracted too, and she wondered if that would be their life. Moments of clarity and peace and togetherness, and then moments of what looked like clouds and maybe storm clouds at that.

She had no one to really talk to about it except Robin, and Ilse didn't want to do that, in case it got back to her brother. Plus, Ilse felt it wasn't fair to Robin or Keith, since they should be able to have their own relationship without Ilse in the middle. Then, at some point, she would just castigate herself for being a fool.

Dennis once again walked past her, tapped her on the shoulder, and said, "Remember. Talk to him."

"Easier said than done," she replied.

"No, all of this,"—he waved his arms around the kitchen—"all of this meandering confusion, all the wondering, all the *what ifs*, and *how tos*," he said, "would *all* clear up if you just talked to him."

"I have to get it straight in my head first," she said mildly.

"No," he said, "you don't." He looked at the menu. "Fish and chips, huh?"

"Yeah. Keith asked for it," she said.

He turned, looked at her, and grinned. "Not bad when one special patient gets to ask for something for everybody."

She flushed and said, "If it puts a smile on his face, then I'm happy."

"Exactly," he said. "So don't feel guilty about it. Just talk to the poor man."

"I'm working on it," she said.

He just gave a hard headshake and walked off.

She didn't want to get sucked up into that whole *what to do* thing, when everything felt so fresh and so new. She knew that Keith was slowly rebuilding his relationship with his sister. Not that it was ever bad, but the two siblings hadn't spent anywhere near enough time together in their adult lives, and this was a great opportunity for that.

Ilse had also seen Keith with Iain earlier, and they appeared to be hitting it off wonderfully. That was something else that she liked because, from what she had seen, Keith didn't make friends easily. Neither did she, for that matter. She had plenty of friendly acquaintances but not so many true friends. Of course she had all the guys and gals she worked with, but she was their boss, so it didn't count.

When lunch rolled around, she stepped out and stood behind the cafeteria line with Dennis, helping to serve. He looked at her a couple times and asked, "What if he doesn't show up?"

"Then he doesn't show up," she said with a smile. "From the reactions of the people so far, fish and chips apparently wasn't a bad idea."

"Isn't that the truth? Several people have been through and just had fish and chips, instead of a mixed plate full of some of it all." When she looked up the next time, Keith walked in the cafeteria door on crutches. He was moving slowly, holding on to the crutches, but also taking several steps without them. When he reached the cafeteria line, she smiled at him. "That's another stage of progress."

"A little scary though," he said. "This is Shane's idea."

"It seems like a good idea," she said. "It's too easy to become so accustomed to having wheelchairs and crutches that we forget we were never meant to use them."

"But falling is not fun," he said, "so it's nice to have something, at least until I have a little more confidence in my legs."

She smiled. He took one look at the food and said, "Fish and chips, huh?"

Such joy was in his voice that Dennis reached over and nudged her. "Just for you," Dennis said in a low voice.

Keith flashed a bright smile at Ilse. "And I certainly will make good use of this opportunity." He quickly reached for five pieces of fish and a few chips.

She laughed. "Hey, we're always looking for good menu ideas," she said.

"Well, you can repeat this anytime," he said. And obviously not able to stop and talk because a crowd formed behind him, Keith flashed her a quick smile and whispered, "Thanks." Then he headed over to a table. When he'd gone by her again to grab coffee, he glanced back and asked, "Join me?"

She looked over at Dennis, who smiled and said, "Go. And take some fish and chips with you." He quickly served her up a dish with the fish, but she stopped him from putting chips on too. Instead she grabbed a Caesar salad and a fork.

Then she headed out to the cafeteria table to spend some

time with Keith. He looked up when he saw her and laughed. "I'm pretty stoked to try this out," he said, gesturing to the fish and chips.

She sat down beside him, content that at least she'd managed to put that smile on his face.

"IT'S DELICIOUS," KEITH said warmly.

"Good," she said. "All I ever wanted to do since I was little was cook."

"That's not the most normal career path for a child," he said, "but I'm grateful you did so well because this is awesome."

"This is simple," she said. "The stuff you have to learn in culinary school? That's a whole different story."

"Well, I, for one, would much rather have a plate of real food like this," he said, "than all that fancy stuff any day."

She said, "You look a little bit better today."

He nodded. "Another one of those mind-bending twists," he said. "I think I even made Shane happy today."

"Is he a taskmaster?"

"He is, and apparently I haven't been completely showing up for the job."

She was surprised that he even mentioned it, and she looked at him in shock. "What does that mean?"

"Apparently I've been holding back, out of some internal fear that truly giving it my all wouldn't get me the results I wanted," he said. "So I've been dogging it, giving myself a fallback excuse."

"Ah, got it," she said. "I did that in school."

He looked at her in surprise.

"I was afraid to challenge those I considered the better students in the class. So, instead of getting grades in the nineties and one hundreds, I would do solid seventies and eighties. It was enough to get me through everything, but it wasn't enough to make me a top student."

"Wow," he said. "I guess that's kind of the same thing. I just hadn't considered that other people were doing it."

"I think it's a self-defense thing," she said. "If I was at the top of the class, everybody would look at me and would judge me that much harder because I would be the best. Turns out everybody wanted to be the best, but nobody wanted to be held to that much higher standard and also be criticized constantly."

He nodded slowly. "And did you finish school that way?"

"No," she said. "My mother told me what I was doing. She showed me how I was doing it and said that maybe, just once, it would be nice to achieve something for myself and that I should put in 100 percent of my effort, not just seventy. The next year I graduated at the top of the class," she said with a laugh, "and I timed it just right, so I could leave in the number one spot, but I didn't have to deal with all the students behind me in the rankings who hated me."

He laughed. "I love it," he said. "That's cool. I guess maybe I've been doing that too. It's a sobering thought though. Using a baseball analogy, if you never take that giant swing at a pitch, you avoid some embarrassing strike-out scene, but you give up the opportunity for that grand slam home run."

"As long as you've learned that lesson," she said firmly, "it doesn't matter now. So, how's the relationship with your sister going?"

"Perfect," he said. "They're making wedding plans. Apparently I'll walk her down the aisle and hand her over to Iain."

"I think that's lovely," she said. "I hadn't heard yet."

"Hey, I just heard it yesterday," he said immediately. "I know she's got a big list of people to invite."

Ilse shrugged. "We're friends, but she may have a lot of other friends too. I don't know."

"I wouldn't worry about it," he said, wondering if he'd accidently crossed some invisible line here.

She laughed and said, "No, don't worry about it. Robin and I are good."

With relief, he attacked the fish again. "I'm so glad to hear that."

"What do you think of Iain?"

"Well, he was at the top of the class, so I hate him," he said cheerfully. Then he watched in joy as she started to laugh, then got the giggles and couldn't stop. He leaned forward and said, "Not really. Obviously I don't hate him. My sister loves him, so that's good enough for me. Iain already knows that, if he does anything to hurt her, I'll be right there, and it's me he'll have to face. Besides, what I've seen of him so far, I like him."

"Typical protective brother," she teased.

"Absolutely, but it's also a good thing," he said. "He may have a line on some work for me."

"Cybersecurity?"

He nodded. "Somebody who's looking at setting up a security company needs a couple pros, one in the cybersecurity field," he said. "I was thinking about setting up my own company, but I'm probably better off to start with somebody else first."

"So does this guy have the money to bankroll this endeavor?"

"Don't know. His name is Gunner," he said with a frown. "I'm not exactly sure about the rest of it, but apparently he's heavily involved in all kinds of things."

"When will you meet him?"

"Well, we've been emailing back and forth already, and he knows that I've got a few more months in here yet, but I'm hopeful."

"So—" and she abruptly stopped, looking embarrassed.

He looked at her, leaned across, and covered her hand with his. "*So* ... what does that mean? Is there something you want to ask me?"

She sighed. "I guess I'm asking," she said, "if you'll be staying in town then."

"Well, that was always the intention," he said. He watched as a tiny smile kicked up at the corner of her mouth. He sat back. "I guess I never said that out loud, did I?"

She shook her head. "I have to admit that I was worried," she confessed.

"Gunner's out of Houston, but he wants to set up a Dallas office." Keith glanced around at all the people seated around them. "You know what? It would be really nice if we could talk somewhere with some privacy for a change."

"Well, tomorrow is Friday," she said. "How would you feel about a picnic?"

He looked at her in delight.

"If you can walk out to the animals, that is."

"I'll make it," he said. "Even if I have to bring the wheelchair, I'll make it."

And, with that, they heard her name called out from the kitchen. She smiled, lifted her empty plate, and said, "Guess

I've got to go."

"Tomorrow then?"

"Tomorrow," she said with a laugh, then headed back to the kitchen.

He sat here with a silly smile on his face and finished off his plate. Dennis appeared almost immediately. Keith looked up, smiled, and said, "That was the best fish and chips I've ever had."

"Well, it was made with love," Dennis said, "so it should have been."

Once he was gone, his words resonated deep inside Keith. Because that's where they were heading. He really cared about her, and, if she cared about him like Dennis just implied, maybe, just maybe, Keith would be the luckiest man in the world. He understood more about what Iain had said earlier because, if Keith had that relationship with Ilse to look forward to, then he also wanted to make sure that he was as strong and as fit and as healthy as he could possibly be. He didn't want his health problems to be any more burdensome than they absolutely had to be. Because that burden would fall on her as well.

And when Keith sought out Shane at the gym later that afternoon, Shane looked up and frowned at him. "What do you want?"

"I want another session."

"What?"

"So, you're right," he said. "I was cheating myself. I hadn't realized it, but now I do." He took a deep breath. "I have something in my future that I really, really, really want to be my best for. And, for that, I need to work harder."

Shane stared at him, and then he started to laugh. "Ilse, by any chance?"

Keith shoved his hands in his pockets and said, "May-be."

"I'm all for having a great relationship as a motivator," Shane said. "God knows I've seen that happen and work time and time again. But what I can't have is you doing this work for her and not for yourself."

"It's not just for her," he said. "It's for me, so I can be the best I can be with her."

Shane pondered it for a moment and then gave a clipped nod. "How are you feeling?"

"Underworked," he said.

Shane hopped to his feet, laughing. "You'll regret those words. Come on. Let's go."

Chapter 15

THE NEXT MORNING Ilse was singing and dancing in the kitchen, having such a hard time containing her joy. The closer it got to lunchtime, the quieter she became. When she started packing up the picnic basket, Dennis came over and double-checked to make sure she had what she needed. He added a bottle of wine and said, "I think you should take two."

"Two baskets? Isn't that overkill?"

He brought over a second basket, quickly repacked it with a blanket on the bottom, then added the wine and wineglasses. In the other basket, he packed up the food. "There."

She looked at it and then at him. "You've done this a time or two."

He grinned and said, "I'm starting to feel a bit like a matchmaker in this place."

She laughed. "If it works, I'm all for it." She kept checking the clock.

"Did you set up a time?" he asked.

She shook her head.

"Well, that was foolish," he said. "Now you'll just keep waiting."

"I know," she said, "and it sucks. Aren't you supposed to be doling out lunch?"

"I am," he said, and he disappeared to help.

As she sat here, she waited and waited and waited.

Dennis poked his head around the corner. "Still no sign of him out here. Why don't you go to his room?"

She frowned.

He shook his head and said, "Remember the benefits of actual communication?"

She nodded, then slipped out the side door and walked toward his room. She knocked on the door, and he called out to come in. When she stepped inside, he sat there, on the bed, rubbing his face. He looked like he'd just woken up.

He looked at her and smiled. "I'm so sorry. I fell asleep."

Immediately her heart calmed down. "That's fine," she said. "Are you still up for a picnic?"

He looked at her in surprise. "Absolutely. Do we have time?"

"I do if you do."

He checked his schedule, nodding, and said, "I've got an hour and a half until my next appointment," he said, "but I am tired, so I'll definitely take the wheelchair." He hopped to his feet, grabbed his crutches, and went to the bathroom. When he came back out, he put the crutches down on the bed and grabbed the wheelchair. "Do you mind?"

"I'll never mind if you use a wheelchair or crutches," she said.

He nodded. "I'm grateful for that too."

They headed out, and she said, "Let's take the elevator."

"Where's the lunch?" he asked.

"I'll be right back," she said with a smile, and she returned to the kitchen, grabbed the baskets, and rejoined him.

When he saw her and both baskets, he said, "Wow, good thing I'm hungry."

"It is, indeed," she said, laughing. She gently put one of the baskets on his lap. "You can carry that one."

He chuckled, and they made their way past the vet clinic and out to the large wide path. She walked beside him as he slowly pushed the wheelchair down the heavily packed gravel walkway. When they got to where the horses were, she wandered around, looking for a spot, then pointed to a nice little low spot over on the left, near the paddock. "What about there?"

Just then, several of the horses came over to greet them. She put the baskets down, opened up the one with the blanket, spread it out, and brought out the wine. Setting the basket to the side, she walked down a few feet to the animals and spent a few moments cuddling them. When she looked over, Keith was at the fence beside her. He was scratching Midnight's beautiful long nose.

"They're so beautiful," he murmured.

"And very understanding," she said. She looked back and saw that he had made his way over without the wheelchair or crutches. "Wow. I hadn't expected to see that either."

"The legs work," he said, "but sometimes they're not something I can really count on."

She turned and headed the few steps over to the blanket where she opened up the other basket. She deliberately left him to his devices to get where he needed to go, using whatever methodology he needed. But when he took two hesitant steps toward the blanket, and then managed to crouch down and sit, she smiled at him. "That was very well done."

He grinned at her. "According to Shane, Dani, and Iain, I still have months and months to go, but I'm beginning to see the progress I need to see." He winced as he shifted.

"Sounds like maybe you're doing too much."

"No," he said. "I'm finally doing the right amount." He didn't explain, and that was okay too.

She laid out the picnic foods and served up two plates of everything.

He looked at the food and smiled. "This looks amazing."

"I hope so," she said. "It's just for us." And she sat here in the beautiful sunshine, watching the horses and the long green grass, feeling happy inside for the first time in a very long while.

KEITH COULDN'T BELIEVE how much effort she'd gone to for him. "You know what? Having a date at a place like this is pretty hard to pull off," he said, "but you managed."

She looked at him in surprise, then smiled and said, "That's what this is, isn't it?"

"Well, we've been having little dates all along," he said. "Lunches and coffee, but this? This is special."

"It is, indeed." She smiled and took another bite.

He hesitated, not sure what he was supposed to say. "I had a phone call with Gunner earlier this morning. We'll go ahead with the job," he said. "I'll work for him. Not while I'm at Hathaway, but he's hoping to have a start date for me in two and a half months."

"That sounds perfect," she said.

He nodded. "I'm pretty happy, I have to admit. Some of the work I can do from home, and some will require me to go to the local office, but we'll see how it goes."

"Well, it gives you a couple months to figure out where

home will be as well."

He nodded. "And you live here on the Hathaway property, don't you?"

She nodded. "I have one of the larger residences," she said. "I've been here since the beginning. It just happened that way."

He nodded but didn't say anything.

She looked over at him. "You've gotten awfully quiet. Is something wrong?"

He looked up at her, smiled, and said, "Not really," he said. "I'm just wondering about my future and about your future."

"Well, I would like to stay here," she said. "There's just so much value in the work I do."

"There is," he said. "So I can either find a place to live on this side of Hathaway near Dallas, so the commute is a little shorter, and maybe you could move in with me," he said.

She stared at him in surprise. "Oh my," she said.

"Or," he said, "I could check out how big your residence is, and maybe I can move in with you and commute when I have to."

"Oh, my goodness." She stared at him, stunned because he was saying the words that she'd wanted to hear but, at the same time, hadn't expected to hear.

He said, "I'm not very good at this. I mean, *really* not good." With a sigh, he pulled out a very tiny thin metal ring. "This is my mother's. I thought Robin would want it, but she told me it makes better sense for me to have it to give to someone special, like Iain would give her an engagement ring. I've just hung on to it all this time. So I know it certainly isn't an engagement ring, no diamond or anything, and it's only a token—and a cheesy token at that. But it's a piece of my mother that I hung on to with my heart, and I haven't been able to let it go. Maybe I can add a diamond to it, signifying you, so there's a piece of you as well. So I was wondering if maybe, sometime down the road—" He heard her catch her breath as she stared at him, tears in the corner of her eyes. And she already had her hand out, her fingers splayed. With a gentle smile, he placed the little band on her ring finger, and he whispered, "Will you marry me?"

Her fingers closed around his in a hard tight grip, and she tugged him forward ever-so-slightly and kissed him.

"Yes," she whispered, just before their lips met. "Double yes."

He wrapped his arms around her and held her tight. "I didn't expect this when I first came here," he said. "And I'm not anywhere near in the shape that I can be, but I'm getting there." He smiled. "So that means you're seeing the worst that you could possibly see, and I can only tell you that it'll get a whole lot better."

She smiled and reached up a hand, gently rubbing her fingers across his cheek, and she whispered, "If this is all there is," she said, "I'm delighted to spend the rest of my life with you. Please don't worry about how good you can be or where you're going because you're no longer alone. This is a journey for the two of us, and we can work it out, no matter what way it goes."

He tilted her chin and kissed her. "Thank you," he whispered. "Thank you for being awake at five o'clock in the morning and showing me that the world wasn't such a lonely place."

She chuckled and whispered back, "You're so welcome. And thank you for letting me know that the world isn't full of short-term relationships. Thank you for showing me that there really is somebody out there for each and every one of us."

Epilogue

LANCE MAYFAIR STARED at the picture from Iain. In fact, there were multiple photos. It's just that none of them were registering as being from his friend. How was it even possible? Iain had left the same VA hospital Lance was in, as a mess. A determined jokester but somebody who would turn his life around. They hadn't talked too long or too deep because it had been painful for them all. But Lance had never really expected to hear from Iain again. Instead, here he was, sending him photos and letting him know that there was life after the VA hospital. Not only life but a crazy-good life. He stared in shock, and then he read the simple message again.

Get here. It'll make all the difference in the world.

Lance quickly responded.

But will it? Or is it just more false hope?

No, it's not false hope.

Just then his phone rang. He picked it up and answered it. "Are you sure? Because, man, these pictures look like they've been seriously edited with Photoshop."

Iain's laughter boomed through the phone. "I know they do," he said, "but I would never steer you wrong. It's a completely different world now. Take a look at that last photo. That's me. That's me right now," he said. "Compare that to where I was when you saw me last."

"It's unbelievable," he said.

"I know. It is unbelievable, but it happened here to me, and you can do it too. Don't mess it up. This is one of the biggest opportunities you'll ever have," he said. "Send in the application, and I'll put in a good word."

And with that, Iain hung up, leaving Lance to his rather dark thoughts. It was hard to be in the same place forever with no progress. The doctors had pretty well decided he was as good as he would get, and that was it, so what would he do with his life? And how was he supposed to deal with that when everything seemed to be so off-kilter?

It's not what he wanted for his life. This isn't what he expected, and now so much anger was inside him that he just didn't know how to deal with it. If he listened to Iain, Lance might have another chance at something more, but that didn't mean that Iain's progress would be the progress Lance would see in himself. And that was one of the hardest things to accept in life.

Realizing that something could work for everybody else, but you were the one exception it wouldn't work for? He didn't want that. He didn't want any more of that same depressing outlook for his future. He missed his music. It had been a large part of his life before the military, and he'd hoped to give it a bigger part in his future. But not since his accident. However, given Iain's photos—could Lance get some of that dream back?

But as he looked at those photos again, a small voice asked if he could take a chance on this. Did he really want to pass up on applying for the one opportunity he had to make a real difference?

And of course he couldn't. He didn't dare pass it up. Because everything in his world was hanging on this one chance. He had quickly followed the link in the email and found the Hathaway House application form. He looked at it, took a deep breath, and quickly downloaded it. If he just filled it out, he could at least say he tried.

With one last look at the photos from Iain, Lance filled out the application. Quickly he opened up an email, attached the application, and sent it in, using Iain's and Jaden's names as his referrals. Because he'd do anything he could to be the man Iain had showed him was possible. Now he just had to hope one more miracle was left for him too.

This concludes Book 11 of Hathaway House: Keith.

Read about Lance: Hathaway House, Book 12

Hathaway House: Lance (Book #12)

Welcome to Hathaway House. Rehab Center. Safe Haven. Second chance at life and love.

Lance Mayfair sought out Hathaway House at the recommendation of a friend, who told him it was an answer to prayer. Lance knows more about prayers than answers, but, if he can see progress in one particular area of his life and health, it will be worth the effort and the pain. He'll do anything he can to play music again. It's all he has left now that his days as a Navy SEAL are over and, with them, any chance of a happy, productive life.

However, the shoulder injury that ended his career pretty much guarantees he'll never play his beloved instruments ever again.

Unless Hathaway House and Jessica can work a miracle.

Jessica has worked with many patients at Hathaway House, but she connects with Lance in a way she didn't with any of the others. She can see the need inside him—his desire to create again, to heal through music. And his goal becomes her goal: to see him play music in his soul again.

Only his music isn't all he wants or needs, and making him happy goes a long way to making her happy, but it's not enough. Both want and need so much more.

Find Book 12 here!

To find out more visit Dale Mayer's website.

http://smarturl.it/DMSLance

Author's Note

Thank you for reading Keith: Hathaway House, Book 11! If you enjoyed the book, please take a moment and leave a short review.

Dear reader,

I love to hear from readers, and you can contact me at my website: www.dalemayer.com or at my Facebook author page. To be informed of new releases and special offers, sign up for my newsletter or follow me on BookBub. And if you are interested in joining Dale Mayer's Reader Group, here is the Facebook sign up page.
https://smarturl.it/DaleMayerFBGroup

Cheers,
Dale Mayer

Get THREE Free Books Now!

Have you met the SEALS of Honor?

SEALs of Honor Books 1, 2, and 3. Follow the stories of brave, badass warriors who serve their country with honor and love their women to the limits of life and death.

Read Mason, Hawk, and Dane right now for FREE.

Go here and tell me where to send them!
http://smarturl.it/EthanBofB

About the Author

Dale Mayer is a USA Today bestselling author best known for her Psychic Visions and Family Blood Ties series. Her contemporary romances are raw and full of passion and emotion (Second Chances, SKIN), her thrillers will keep you guessing (By Death series), and her romantic comedies will keep you giggling (It's a Dog's Life and Charmin Marvin Romantic Comedy series).

She honors the stories that come to her – and some of them are crazy and break all the rules and cross multiple genres!

To go with her fiction, she also writes nonfiction in many different fields with books available on resume writing, companion gardening and the US mortgage system. She has recently published her Career Essentials Series. All her books are available in print and ebook format.

Connect with Dale Mayer Online

Dale's Website – www.dalemayer.com

Facebook Personal – https://smarturl.it/DaleMayerFacebook

Instagram – https://smarturl.it/DaleMayerInstagram

BookBub – https://smarturl.it/DaleMayerBookbub

Facebook Fan Page – https://smarturl.it/DaleMayerFBFanPage

Goodreads – https://smarturl.it/DaleMayerGoodreads

Also by Dale Mayer

Published Adult Books:

Hathaway House

Aaron, Book 1

Brock, Book 2

Cole, Book 3

Denton, Book 4

Elliot, Book 5

Finn, Book 6

Gregory, Book 7

Heath, Book 8

Iain, Book 9

Jaden, Book 10

Keith, Book 11

Lance, Book 12

The K9 Files

Ethan, Book 1

Pierce, Book 2

Zane, Book 3

Blaze, Book 4

Lucas, Book 5

Parker, Book 6

Carter, Book 7

Weston, Book 8

Greyson, Book 9

Rowan, Book 10

Lovely Lethal Gardens

Arsenic in the Azaleas, Book 1

Bones in the Begonias, Book 2

Corpse in the Carnations, Book 3

Daggers in the Dahlias, Book 4

Evidence in the Echinacea, Book 5

Footprints in the Ferns, Book 6

Gun in the Gardenias, Book 7

Handcuffs in the Heather, Book 8

Ice Pick in the Ivy, Book 9

Jewels in the Juniper, Book 10

Killer in the Kiwis, Book 11

Psychic Vision Series

Tuesday's Child

Hide 'n Go Seek

Maddy's Floor

Garden of Sorrow

Knock Knock...

Rare Find

Eyes to the Soul

Now You See Her

Shattered

Into the Abyss

Seeds of Malice

Eye of the Falcon

Itsy-Bitsy Spider

Unmasked

Deep Beneath

From the Ashes

Stroke of Death

Psychic Visions Books 1–3

Psychic Visions Books 4–6
Psychic Visions Books 7–9

By Death Series

Touched by Death
Haunted by Death
Chilled by Death
By Death Books 1–3

Broken Protocols – Romantic Comedy Series

Cat's Meow
Cat's Pajamas
Cat's Cradle
Cat's Claus
Broken Protocols 1-4

Broken and... Mending

Skin
Scars
Scales (of Justice)
Broken but… Mending 1-3

Glory

Genesis
Tori
Celeste
Glory Trilogy

Biker Blues

Morgan: Biker Blues, Volume 1
Cash: Biker Blues, Volume 2

SEALs of Honor

Mason: SEALs of Honor, Book 1

Hawk: SEALs of Honor, Book 2
Dane: SEALs of Honor, Book 3
Swede: SEALs of Honor, Book 4
Shadow: SEALs of Honor, Book 5
Cooper: SEALs of Honor, Book 6
Markus: SEALs of Honor, Book 7
Evan: SEALs of Honor, Book 8
Mason's Wish: SEALs of Honor, Book 9
Chase: SEALs of Honor, Book 10
Brett: SEALs of Honor, Book 11
Devlin: SEALs of Honor, Book 12
Easton: SEALs of Honor, Book 13
Ryder: SEALs of Honor, Book 14
Macklin: SEALs of Honor, Book 15
Corey: SEALs of Honor, Book 16
Warrick: SEALs of Honor, Book 17
Tanner: SEALs of Honor, Book 18
Jackson: SEALs of Honor, Book 19
Kanen: SEALs of Honor, Book 20
Nelson: SEALs of Honor, Book 21
Taylor: SEALs of Honor, Book 22
Colton: SEALs of Honor, Book 23
Troy: SEALs of Honor, Book 24
Axel: SEALs of Honor, Book 25
SEALs of Honor, Books 1–3
SEALs of Honor, Books 4–6
SEALs of Honor, Books 7–10
SEALs of Honor, Books 11–13
SEALs of Honor, Books 14–16
SEALs of Honor, Books 17–19

Heroes for Hire

Levi's Legend: Heroes for Hire, Book 1
Stone's Surrender: Heroes for Hire, Book 2
Merk's Mistake: Heroes for Hire, Book 3
Rhodes's Reward: Heroes for Hire, Book 4
Flynn's Firecracker: Heroes for Hire, Book 5
Logan's Light: Heroes for Hire, Book 6
Harrison's Heart: Heroes for Hire, Book 7
Saul's Sweetheart: Heroes for Hire, Book 8
Dakota's Delight: Heroes for Hire, Book 9
Michael's Mercy (Part of Sleeper SEAL Series)
Tyson's Treasure: Heroes for Hire, Book 10
Jace's Jewel: Heroes for Hire, Book 11
Rory's Rose: Heroes for Hire, Book 12
Brandon's Bliss: Heroes for Hire, Book 13
Liam's Lily: Heroes for Hire, Book 14
North's Nikki: Heroes for Hire, Book 15
Anders's Angel: Heroes for Hire, Book 16
Reyes's Raina: Heroes for Hire, Book 17
Dezi's Diamond: Heroes for Hire, Book 18
Vince's Vixen: Heroes for Hire, Book 19
Ice's Icing: Heroes for Hire, Book 20
Johan's Joy: Heroes for Hire, Book 21
Galen's Gemma: Heroes for Hire, Book 22
Heroes for Hire, Books 1–3
Heroes for Hire, Books 4–6
Heroes for Hire, Books 7–9
Heroes for Hire, Books 10–12
Heroes for Hire, Books 13–15

SEALs of Steel

Badger: SEALs of Steel, Book 1

Erick: SEALs of Steel, Book 2
Cade: SEALs of Steel, Book 3
Talon: SEALs of Steel, Book 4
Laszlo: SEALs of Steel, Book 5
Geir: SEALs of Steel, Book 6
Jager: SEALs of Steel, Book 7
The Final Reveal: SEALs of Steel, Book 8
SEALs of Steel, Books 1–4
SEALs of Steel, Books 5–8
SEALs of Steel, Books 1–8

The Mavericks

Kerrick, Book 1
Griffin, Book 2
Jax, Book 3
Beau, Book 4
Asher, Book 5
Ryker, Book 6
Miles, Book 7
Nico, Book 8
Keane, Book 9
Lennox, Book 10
Gavin, Book 11
Shane, Book 12

Bullard's Battle Series

Ryland's Reach, Book 1
Cain's Cross, Book 2
Eton's Escape, Book 3
Garret's Gambit, Book 4
Kano's Keep, Book 5
Fallon's Flaw, Book 6
Quinn's Quest, Book 7

Bullard's Beauty, Book 8

Collections

Dare to Be You…

Dare to Love…

Dare to be Strong…

RomanceX3

Standalone Novellas

It's a Dog's Life

Riana's Revenge

Second Chances

Published Young Adult Books:

Family Blood Ties Series

Vampire in Denial

Vampire in Distress

Vampire in Design

Vampire in Deceit

Vampire in Defiance

Vampire in Conflict

Vampire in Chaos

Vampire in Crisis

Vampire in Control

Vampire in Charge

Family Blood Ties Set 1–3

Family Blood Ties Set 1–5

Family Blood Ties Set 4–6

Family Blood Ties Set 7–9

Sian's Solution, A Family Blood Ties Series Prequel Novelette

Design series

Dangerous Designs

Deadly Designs

Darkest Designs

Design Series Trilogy

Standalone

In Cassie's Corner

Gem Stone (a Gemma Stone Mystery)

Time Thieves

Published Non-Fiction Books:

Career Essentials

Career Essentials: The Résumé

Career Essentials: The Cover Letter

Career Essentials: The Interview

Career Essentials: 3 in 1

Printed in Great Britain
by Amazon